P9-CMW-438

little white lies

little white lies

Brianna Baker

F. Bowman Hastie III

SOHO
TEEN

Copyright © 2016 Brianna Baker, F. Bowman Hastie III, and Soho Press

All rights reserved.

This is a work of fiction. Names, characters, places, and incidents either are the product of the author's imagination or are used fictitiously, and any resemblance to actual persons, living or dead, businesses, companies, events, or locales is entirely coincidental.

Published in the United States by Soho Teen
an imprint of
Soho Press, Inc.
853 Broadway
New York, NY 10003

Library of Congress Cataloging-in-Publication Data

Baker, Brianna.
Little white lies / Brianna Baker & F. Bowman Hastie III.

ISBN 978-1-61695-707-0
eISBN 978-1-61695-516-8

1. Tumblr (Electronic resource)—Fiction. 2. Microblogs—Fiction.
3. Fame—Fiction. 4. Friendship—Fiction. 5. African Americans—Fiction.
6. Humorous stories. I. Hastie, F. Bowman. II. Title.
PZ7.1.B34Li 2016
[Fic]—dc23 2015020055

Interior design by Janine Agro, Soho Press, Inc.

Printed in the United States of America

10 9 8 7 6 5 4 3 2 1

For Phyllis, Teresa, Wayne and my Kelly. Also for those who wandered off the beaten path. From what I can tell, the extra dirt is worth it.
—Brianna Baker

little white lies

OFFICIAL *LITTLE WHITE LIES* DISCLAIMER

DEAR READER,
PLEASE NOTE PRIOR TO PROCEEDING WITH THE REST OF THIS BOOK:

THIS IS A WORK OF **FICTION**. THE MAIN CHARACTERS IN THIS WORK OF FICTION ARE PURELY **FICTIONAL**. HOWEVER, THESE **FICTIONAL** CHARACTERS EXIST IN A WORLD THAT ALSO INCLUDES **PEOPLE WHO EXIST IN REAL LIFE** (E.G., KANYE WEST, CORNEL WEST, ADAM WEST*). FOR THE SAKE OF OUR BOOK WE HAVE INCLUDED **FICTIONAL** ACTIONS BY "REAL LIFE" PEOPLE. **WE ASSURE YOU THAT ANY FICTIONAL ACTIONS BY "REAL LIFE" PEOPLE WITHIN THIS WORK OF FICTION ARE PURELY FICTIONAL AND HAVE NO RELATION TO THE "REAL LIFE" ACTIONS OF THESE PEOPLE IN REAL LIFE.** WE LOVE YOU, WESTS!

—THE AUTHORS

*No version—fictional or nonfictional—of TV's original Batman, Adam West, appears in this book, except within the disclaimer above and in this footnote.

PROLOGUE

January 8, 2014

from: Coretta <coretta.white@gmail.com>

to: Mom, Dad, Mike, Rachel, Karin Skool, Anders Skool, Douglas Cornelius, Esther Cornelius, Alex Melrose, Karl Ristoff

date: Tue, January 7, 2014 at 7:17 p.m.

subject: Confidential

Dear Valued Friend, Colleague, or Loved One whose trust I've betrayed:

I am writing this letter to you with a very heavy heart.

My confession: I, Coretta White, am not the author of every post on *Little White Lies*. For the past twelve weeks, I have been receiving assistance from a ghostwriter. You all know me to be a proud young woman who was raised to uphold a certain code of ethics. Today I must admit to you all—and most importantly, to myself—that I betrayed this code.

At the beginning of my senior year, I felt as much on top of the world as I felt crushed by the weight of it. *Little White Lies* exploded the way viral things do, I guess, without warning and without any real reason, as far as I can tell. I mean, yes, it was funny and struck a nerve. But suddenly it was huge, and the explosion consumed me. It kept me from college applications, student council president duties, Spanish club president duties, law club president duties, upkeep of my hair (I know you noticed), and just being a good friend and girlfriend.

While I thought my unraveling was going unnoticed, I was wrong. My most trusted source for just about everything knew I was suffering. So she approached me with an offer to lighten my workload. This led me to the services of Karl Ristoff, who helped me "keep up" with *Little White Lies*.

Looking back, I am not quite sure why I thought that having a forty-one-year-old white man ghostwriting for me would help. But here we are.

As much as I hate to admit it, once Karl took over *Little White Lies*, the blog went to a whole new level. You all know that it started as a way for me to laugh at my parents' hasty generalizations. But then my teachers started cutting me slack. Then I was offered my own show on Pulse TV. Not to mention getting numerous perks that a seventeen-year-old would never dream of (well, maybe Beyoncé at seventeen).

It started with Karl and me working in tandem. But it quickly veered toward becoming *The Karl Show*. I am to blame for that. And in the end, I know that my success wouldn't have happened if it weren't for Karl.

At the start of my senior year, my biggest fear was that I would fail and let all of you down. That I wasn't really as smart and talented as everyone thought I was or should be. That eventually one of the several plates that I was spinning would fall. That something would expose me for the impostor that I am.

What irony that this fear is what led me to *become* an impostor.

I would ask that you please find it in your heart to forgive me, as I, too, work to forgive myself.

With love and regret,
Coretta White

Part One: Fall 2013

CHAPTER ONE

Karl (November 20, 2013)

When the Real Money Phone rang that day, I knew the job was important, whatever it was. R$$P: the gold iPhone 5S with the Pink Floyd* ringtone. As opposed to the Fake Money Phone—F$$P—recently upgraded to a slime-green 5C but still with the "Two Tickets to Paradise"* ring. Hey, I've always liked to stay current, even while insisting that certain things never change.

More on my money phones—fake and real—later.

(Also, if you don't get my cultural references*, that's your failing. This handy asterisk, presuming failure, will urge you to consult Appendix 1 on page 243, or proceed to your preferred Internet browser for further information.)

I stared at the glowing face of Tony Robbins as he vibrated on my tidy communications table: a battered door resting on the tops of two stumpy old filing cabinets. Tony Robbins and Pink Floyd, what a winning combination. Once the bass line was established and the guitars came in, I reached for R$$P and went to speakerphone. Tony Robbins disappeared along with his smile, mere wallpaper. He never calls. Honestly, I'm not even sure who he is.

"Bueno," I answered, in the style of Mexicans.

"Carlito!"

It was Alex, of course, the only person on the planet who had the R$$P number. She'd given the phone to me.

I honestly don't like talking on phones at all. One reason I insist on speakerphone is because it annoys the caller, thereby shortening the call and discouraging the caller from calling again in the future.

With texts and emails, I respond immediately and without fail.

I refuse to listen to voicemail. Therefore I never leave voicemail for others. I try to be consistent, and within reason, considerate.

Oh, and just for the record, I've never done FaceTime and never been in a Google Hangout, and I intend to experience neither during this lifetime. Not that there's anything wrong with it . . .

When a Money Phone rings, I always answer. Even F$$P. But everyone—including Alex, to whom I owe my life and my livelihood—gets put on speaker.

"Hey, Al. What's shakin'?"

"Karl, am I on speakerphone?"

"Yes."

"Take me off, please."

"Alex, darling." I assumed one of my hackneyed accents, a treacly Anglo lilt I vaguely associate with Errol Flynn*. "You know that when I touch my iPhone with any part of my body, the likelihood of my losing your call goes up astronomically."

At the time, my communications table accommodated these two iPhones, an iPad, a Samsung Galaxy tablet, a MacBook Air laptop, and my cable and Wi-Fi setup. Still, the reception in my Bed-Stuy basement was deplorable. Another reason I hated talking on the phone.

"Okay, whatever." Alex always caved in to the speaker-phone, but never without a fight. "Are you alone?"

"Of course I'm alone. I'm always alone, babe. Ever since you walked out on me all those years ago."

"Hey, buddy, you walked out on me, remember?"

"Ah, righto." I resumed my Errol Flynn lilt. "So I did. But you didn't exactly beg me to take you back, now did you, buttercup?"

"No, I did not, Karl." Alex delivered her line as if part of a well-rehearsed repartee, which in a way it was. "But I did insist that we remain friends, did I not?"

"Yes, you did, dear friend."

"Even though *you* insisted that staying friends with exes was only, as you put it, 'for sissies and sword swallowers.'"

"Ah, sissies and sword swallowers." My inflection made the words sing. "Did I say that, love? I haven't the foggiest clue as to what it even means."

The truth: in spite of occasional doubts, staying friends with Alex was the best decision I had ever made in my life.

Alex Melrose and I dated for thirteen weeks, which seemed like a really long time during college. Come to think of it, she was my first bona fide girlfriend at Harvard, and we didn't even hook up until spring semester of our senior year. Or rather, *my* senior year. Al was finishing the first year of her MBA.

We made sense. We liked the same stoner movies and the same twisted cartoons. We loved beer. We loved it in a way that we felt made us superior to others who loved beer. We laughed a lot, mostly at others' expense. We had tons of fun. But fooling around never quite felt right. I suppose you could say we had intimacy issues. It's hard to explain, but every time we made out I felt like I was kissing my stepsister or something.

Having sex wasn't much better. I mean, it was better. Because we were having sex. And I was really happy to be having sex with anybody, especially someone as smart and funny and beautiful as Alex Melrose. Someone I genuinely liked.

But whenever we finished, I felt as if I had just had sex with my stepsister. Not a sin. Not entirely deplorable or completely disgusting. Just wrong.

After thirteen weeks—a whole semester—I walked out on her. Or rather, broke up with her over coffee in a diner without giving much of an explanation.

I don't believe in giving explanations when breaking up. It never feels like anything I could say would do either party good. So I say as little as possible.

Alex told me she wouldn't insist on hearing my reasons for breaking up as long as I promised that we would remain friends. Forever. She knew me well enough to know that if I made that vow to her, I wouldn't break it. I would keep my vow for the same reason I broke up with her: it would be wrong to do otherwise.

And so here we were.

"You're right; that was a long time ago, Karl. And now I've got a job for you." Alex was back to all business.

I groaned, even though I'd been waiting for her to get to the point. "Another job? I got enough jobs already!"

"Oh, I know you do, believe me. You're King Twit, Dark Lord of the Twitterverse." Alex probably thought she was massaging my massive ego. "But this isn't just another ghost-tweet gig."

I sprang up on the big silver exercise ball that functioned as my office chair. "Now you're talking."

"I know you're suffering from some form of Twitter exhaustion, Karl. I can see it in your tweets."

I quickly turned defensive. "Have there been complaints?"

"No, Karl. No complaints from clients. Not lately." Alex took on a reassuring tone. "But I know you've been wanting to get back into longer-form writing. And besides, Twitter is not exactly the future."

"It's a lot trickier to ghost an Instagram."

"Not that there won't be tweeting involved with this new gig," Alex continued. "But if you play your cards right, you may be able to let the rest of your top twits go."

"You mean, only work for this one client? You know I don't do exclusives."

"Well, I'm sure you would consider it if I could only tell you who's footing the bill." Alex switched into smug mode. "She's richer than God."

"Who is it?"

"Sorry, can't tell you."

"What does she do?"

"She owns her own network."

Before I could utter, "Oh," Alex cut me off.

"Not Oprah."

"Not Oprah?" I was at a loss. "Who else could it be?"

"You know I can't tell you, Karl. All I can say is, not Oprah."

"Okaaaayyyy. So Noprah, that's cool. Can't tell me who the client is, not a problem. Richer than God? I'm in."

"Great. Now we've just got to put you in touch with Coretta . . ."

Given who Noprah probably was, my mind only went to one place. "Coretta White?" I asked.

Alex laughed. "You've heard of her?" Now *she* was surprised.

"Of course I've heard of her. *Little White Lies*. That's my shit!"

CHAPTER TWO

Coretta (September 9–10, 2013)

tumblr.
LITTLE WHITE LIES

September 9, 2013

Little White Lie of the Day: Dante de Blasio, the fifteen-year-old son of New York mayoral candidate Bill de Blasio, should "really shave that Afro down if he knows what is good for him and for his father's campaign."

Dear Friends, Countrymen, and Strangers,

Today I write from my dining room table. It is 7:15 A.M. on a humid Monday morning in Brooklyn. Now you might ask yourself, why is it so damn humid in Brooklyn today? And why is a well-adjusted seventeen-year-old girl hastily blogging for the first time in her life?

While I can't speak to the weather, though global warming is likely to blame, I'm writing this because I've been pushed to the brink this morning. Pushed to the brink of my sanity by the ones that brought me into this world.

While I do still hold to the notion that (most) parents (usually) know best, I do think there are (A LOT of) exceptions.

I can no longer idly sit by and consume the Little White Lies that my parents tell me each and every day.

I know they don't mean any harm, just as Miley Cyrus doesn't when she walks outside each and every day without pants. Nonetheless, the harm is still being done.

Today, while I squeezed frosting onto a nutritionally void, overcooked, yet somehow also half-frozen toaster strudel, a political ad featuring Dante de Blasio appeared on our kitchen TV.

Dante is the handsome, fifteen-year-old (biracial) son of the white (errr . . . Caucasian) New York mayoral candidate Bill de Blasio. In the ad, Dante sports a rather fierce Afro and speaks against the NYPD stop-and-frisk policy.

If you don't know the ad, get with the program and YouTube it.

My father's response? Dante "really should shave that Afro if he knows what is good for him and for his father's campaign."

My mother's response? She agreed with him.

Their justification: a fifteen-year-old's Afro provides a reason for the city of New York (Bloomberg and the Snooze Brigade) to defend the NYPD police officers' right to profile (based on Afros, of course), and to "stop and frisk" anyone at any time for any reason. Including Afros.

I can't. I just can't.

I would like us all to take a moment and ask ourselves a very important question: Is this what Rosa Parks would have done? Would she have said, "Hey, you know what? You're right; I think I *will* give up my seat on the bus after all. It makes sense because Montgomery did pass a city ordinance in 1900, a city I'm not even allowed to vote in, that said bus drivers can make me give up my seat to white (err . . . Caucasian) people."

In case you're Googling: 1.) No, she did not say that. 2.) You're an idiot. 3.) Throw your computer out the window, because nothing can save you. 4.) I'm paraphrasing above, but yes, Montgomery (the state capital of Alabama) did pass such an ordinance in 1900.

It may be 2013, and I might have the right to sit in a pee-ridden MTA seat just like anybody else, but the issue remains the same. Dante's Afro isn't just a handy excuse to get fondled by the police. It's a bus seat in Montgomery, Alabama. People need to see this white mayoral candidate in a commercial with his (dare I say) handsome African-American son.

WITH HIS AFRO.

They need to see that this young man is smart. He is aware that his father is a white politician, and he is also aware that when he is not with his father, he is just another young black man. *That* is what's good for Dante's father—and for his campaign. That is where progress and change are born. It is inspiring. In fact, it makes me want to have an Afro of my own.

Disclaimer: I would have to shave my head to grow a respectable Afro, because I would need to get the perm out of my hair first (African-American perm, not Julia Roberts perm). This isn't something I can tackle my senior year of high school, but know that it's now on my list.

What are the takeaways from this early morning rant?
1. Eat something for breakfast that wasn't created in a lab.
2. Loving your parents doesn't mean they can't be wrong.
3. Roll your eyes like no one is watching. But they always are.
4. Dante de Blasio, call me in five years.

5. And for God's sake, make sure that your subway seat isn't wet before you sit down.

It wasn't even 8 A.M., and I'd already commented on five Facebook statuses, eaten a garbage breakfast, and written my very first blog post. All while my parents sat at the table and stared at their iPads. Ah, modern technology, you've really let the family unit disconnect from each other. Something every teenager is supremely grateful for.

Keys, homework, gum, phone, laptop. According to Google Maps, I had six minutes to get to the train, which really meant I had five.

"Gotta go. See you guys tonight," I mumbled, halfway to the door.

My father is not a fan of my "I'm a teen on the go" routine. He watched me fumble with my backpack, smirking. My parents, you see, don't fumble with anything. They are clean-cut and put together. Everything that they do, they do with purpose. I knew Dad had already been up for two hours, worked out, ironed his new suit, and made breakfast, all while looking like a J.Crew model. Ahem, an old J.Crew model, of course.

"Coretta, do you have anything you'd like to say before you just march out of the house?" he asked.

"Umm . . . bye?"

"Very funny," my mother chimed in. "When are you coming home? What do you have after school?"

"I have Spanish club from three to four, and I'm volunteering at SKOOLS 4 ALL from four to six. And yes, I'll be riding the train with Rachel tonight, so don't worry."

Both my mother and father were aware that "volunteering at SKOOLS 4 ALL" was code for "hanging out with my boyfriend Mike." It's not that we *weren't* doing volunteer work or anything; it's just that we were also doing a fair amount of making out basically anywhere we could. Either way, it was going on my college applications. (Not the making-out part.) Call it a draw.

"I really do have to go, though," I said.

My mother really, *really* isn't a fan of my "I'm a teen on the go" routine.

People always tell me I look like her, but I don't think my eyebrows have the power of judgment that hers do. She's not J.Crew striking. She could be pulled from a JCPenney catalogue: pretty, poised, and maybe milquetoast. This is misleading. Get my mother into a debate, and you will lose.

"You know, Coretta, you should wake up earlier if you need more time to get organized in the morning," she said. She finally lifted her eyes from her iPad.

Right after she glared at me, she gazed at my dad, all gooey like they were my age. I could tell she thought he looked cute in his new suit. Gross.

And let's all take into account that my mother has tried to get me to wake up earlier since I was in preschool. It's not in the cards.

"I know, I know, I love you both dearly. I'll be home at six thirty."

I'm supposed to hate Mondays, but there is secretly a part of me that loves them. There, I said it. I love going back to school after a weekend away. I love *school*. I love succeeding. I love excelling. I love being in clubs. I love studying ruthlessly for an exam and showing up knowing I'm going to destroy it. Furthermore, I love being handed back said exam and looking at the "A+" scribbled in red pen next to my name.

I wouldn't say I'm the smartest kid at Booker T. Washington High, not even close. But I can't think of anyone who works harder. For that, I can thank Martin and Felicia White. They instilled in me the satisfaction that comes with earning success. They also taught me that the first thing one should do when one wakes up is brush one's teeth. Like them, I don't understand waiting until after you eat. It's just gross.

I beelined to my locker as the first bell rang.

Waiting for me was my girl Rachel Bernstein in her usual uniform. By that I mean she looked like she was wearing an *actual school uniform*. Rachel had an inexplicable obsession with polos and khaki skirts, all terrible, no matter what the color or style. You'd think I would've given her hell about her clothing choices, but I've learned to choose my battles. I won the hair war. Three years ago, with some gentle persuasion from me, Rachel agreed that her Jew-fro could use a little taming. Unlike Dante de Blasio's, that was a 'fro I could get up in arms about. It was definitely not good for her or her future.

Rachel and I have been friends since we were born, as much as babies can be friends. Her parents met my parents at a town hall meeting about stop signs during the Dinkins administration. They have our family over for Hanukkah celebrations, and we invite them over for Christmas. We had a Kwanzaa celebration one year, but we were all a little confused and decided to just not do that ever again.

Uniformed Rachel got right into it: "I thought you were going to be late or something, and I was going to just go to class, but then I thought that maybe you wouldn't be late. Then I was going to text you, but then I thought I'd just wait."

She has a tendency to ramble, especially on a Monday

morning. But she was chewing on one of her ringlets of hair. So she was nervous about *something*.

"Mondays, right?" I don't know why I insist on saying contrived phrases in a semi-serious way.

"So . . . are you going to talk about this post, or what?"

"Post of . . ."

"Oh, come on, the *Little White Lies* Tumblr! I mean, you didn't tell me you were starting a blog! Then I thought that maybe you were doing it for college applications."

Wait, how did she know about *Little White Lies*? I'd *just* posted that.

I must have been frowning because she smiled. "Coretta, it's really, really good. What made you write that?"

I shrugged. "My parents were getting on my nerves. I don't know, it's probably stupid." Let's be very clear, I did not think the *Little White Lies* post was stupid in any way. But I also didn't really know what to say about it. I honestly didn't think anyone would read it. I'd just needed to vent.

"Stupid? Are you kidding me? It's amazing. It's funny. And dare I say . . . poignant?"

Coming from anyone else, this would sound like bullshit. But Rachel has a tendency to *attempt* to soften blows. In eighth grade, I made a papier-mâché art project that went a bit off the rails: an ode to the underappreciated earthworm. It ended up looking like male genitalia. When I voiced my concerns to her, she said I was crazy. "Of course it looks like an earthworm!" Yet for some middle school idiots, I was Coretta Cock-Ring for the rest of the year.

I managed to smile back. "Well, thanks, girl."

"Coretta, you already have five hundred followers on your Tumblr. I've been writing a fashion blog for two years, and I have thirty-seven." (As you might imagine, her "fashion" blog is a topic of conversation I prefer to avoid.) She pulled out her phone and started scrolling through the list. "Oh, and I sent it to Mike."

Another trait of Rachel's: she has a tendency to overshare, especially with things that aren't hers to share. She is one of those wonderful people born without a filter. I think this is the main reason she's never had a boyfriend. (Not that I've shared that with her. I *do* have a filter.)

As if on cue, my boyfriend turned the corner with his harem of cheerleaders and crew of jocks.

Here I must offer another contrived phrase in a semi-serious way: Mike Cornelius is tall, dark, and handsome. There's no better way to put it. He's the kind of guy who would be cast as a vampire in a teen movie. And as much as I'm against Barbie and the message she sends to young children, Mike would be the prototype for a Ken doll. A black Ken doll.

Whenever Mike walked around with that group, I couldn't help but wonder if any of them were aware of how ridiculous the whole "we play sports, and *we* cheer for them; thusly we walk together" routine was. I wanted to believe that he knew. Like me, Mike comes from a family that prizes academics over athletics. But Mike's family could also probably afford to buy the Brooklyn Nets. And while I'm not into jocks per se, I do like the look of a letterman's jacket.

What I really love about Mike is that he's a not-so-secret nerd.

I'd always known who Mike Cornelius was, but we met at a SKOOLS 4 ALL fundraiser over the summer. Mike was running all of the techy-related things, coordinating the donations on several laptops at once. SKOOLS 4 ALL was a brand-new nonprofit aimed at providing education for children in impoverished African countries, launched with a lot of hype, so Mike had a pretty important job for a seventeen-year-old. He got it because 1) he has the skills and 2) his parents are on the board of Pulse TV, the TV network owned and operated by Karin and Anders Skool—or as they are universally known on Page Six, the Skool Twins.

Pulse TV is kind of a CNN meets MTV (minus the music) for young people. News and pop culture and social issues. When they started, they were cool because they didn't try very hard to brand themselves. Sort of like what *VICE* could be if they were less annoying and had a conscience. Pulse broadcast a lot about the Skool twins themselves, how they were helping with some inner city cause or raising money for some sort of positive global initiative. Hence, SKOOLS 4 ALL. From Pulse TV I learned that ninety-nine percent of all schools in Ethiopia don't even have books. Seriously. A school with no books. WTF?

And the Skools are a pretty interesting pair, to say the least. The Internet says they're twenty-eight, but they could be anywhere from twenty to thirty-five. (I'm not good at ages.) Both are tall and thin, with alabaster hair and skin. High-fashion good looks—you know, from one angle you aren't sure which one is the boy or the girl.

"Babe, this post you wrote about de Blasio is incredible," Mike said to me. "You're so right. I don't even remember how I found it." He had an unfortunate tendency to forget all interactions with Rachel. He also seemed to have forgotten she was standing right in front of him. "You never told me you were a writer!"

Before I could respond, he planted a kiss on me. A public

display of affection, or PDA as the kids were calling it, was really out of the ol' box for Mike Cornelius. *Little White Lies* had really affected him that much? I almost felt like I should plant a kiss on Rachel. For once her oversharing had paid off.

"Maybe now you won't need to call Dante de Blasio in five years," he added with a crooked smirk.

"Are you jealous of Dante, Mike? I just put that in there because you know what they say, sex sells."

He planted one more kiss on me and peeled out like it was choreographed.

Rachel rolled her eyes.

I stood there, blushing, flattered, unable to do anything but giggle like an idiot.

The rest of the day became a blur of compliments and updates from kids around school. By the final bell, *Little White Lies* had over a thousand followers. Don't get me wrong; I knew I had a lot to say, and that I could be entertaining when forced . . . but entertaining to a thousand people, almost all of whom were total strangers?

When I went to sleep, the number was up to 1,342.

I woke up the next morning in a bit of a haze. The day before felt like a dream. I decided not to think about the Tumblr—until, of course, my mother opened her mouth at breakfast.

"Kanye West doesn't know the first thing about fashion." She was on the iPad, scrolling through the latest article featuring one of Kanye's rants.

My mother's morning reading routine ostensibly revolved around reputable sites like CNN or *The New York Times*, but that was just to cover her gossipy tracks. She always made her way to the entertainment section within three minutes.

My dad inevitably glanced away from his physical copy of the *Times*, just to "take a peek" at what the celebrities and youth of America were up to.

"Kanye is such a smart young man, but he is getting involved in things that really don't concern him," he said.

My first inclination was to get into a debate about Kanye. But why bother? Over the course of my seventeen years on Earth, I've found that getting into arguments with a mother who's a professor and a father who's a litigator is a complete waste of time. At least, arguing face-to-face . . . but writing about it? If I'd learned anything from yesterday's surreal experience, blogging was worth my while.

tumblr.
LITTLE WHITE LIES

September 10, 2013

Little White Lie of the Day: Kanye West doesn't know the first thing about fashion.

Mom and Dad, I pity you.

While I will concede that Kanye is an eccentric egomaniac, there is a reason for that. Kanye has built an empire. *Yeezus*, his last album, made Jay Z's *Magna Carta Holy Grail* seem like a track from Paris Hilton's latest garbage bin of supposed "music."

I could have told my mother that this is an artist who wrote a song called "New Slaves." I could have said that it's an eloquent meditation on how the United States is using prison as a way to enslave African-Americans all over again. By increasing the prison time on charges commonly associated with the black community (e.g., crack cocaine, and not meth), new slaves are being stripped of freedom.

Kanye takes hip-hop beyond Benzes and bitches. But yes, there still are Benzes and bitches in there, too.

My mother might then say, "Well, Coretta, we are talking about fashion, not music."

Yes, I agree. We are. I'm not calling him the next Anna Wintour. But he could have a whole team of people create a marketable line, something safe, something he could put his face on. Why are people so mad about Kanye dabbling in things that he "shouldn't"?

Granted, he's with Kim Kardashian. I don't really think I need to say any more about that. But as for the bigger reason, why not look to Yeezus himself? Kanye speaks to society's continual state of agitation and unrest. We aren't at a Code Red but a perpetual Code Orange. This is at the root of so much road rage, jealousy, racism, colorism, classism, etc.

Maybe I'm writing this blog in a state of Code Orange.

Does Kanye need to stop comparing Kim Kardashian to Marilyn Monroe? Perhaps. Could he refer to himself as a "genius" a little less often in casual conversation? Surely. Should he stop pushing the boundaries of music, and if he so desires, fashion? And stop calling out the societal foundations still in place in America, designed to keep African-Americans where we are?

No. Never. Sometimes a Code Orange is necessary.

Three minutes after I uploaded the second post, I got a text from Mike.

> Hey- can i see u before school? I need to talk to u. Meet by your locker? See u soon.

Anytime someone—not just my boyfriend, *anyone*—asks if they can talk to me, my mind goes to terrible places. What could he want to talk to me about? Is he afraid I'm going to shave my head and grow that Afro? Does he want to break up? No. There was no reason for us to break up. I was being crazy, right?

I texted him back.

> Talk? Sure. I'll be at my locker!

During my mini freak-out, I ignored a barrage of texts from Rachel. As someone who overshares, she is a person who likes to send texts in fives. I skipped to the last one.

> LOL! This one was even better!
> I sent it to my parents!

Why? Why did Rachel send this to her parents? If the Bernsteins knew, my parents would now know, too. And while they have some sense of humor, they might not be as amused if they found themselves the catalyst, inspiration, and punching bag for my blog.

Another text from Rachel came in.

> My parents loved it!

Hmm. If they loved it, maybe my parents might? Wishful thinking.

I made a point of smiling cheerfully as I closed my laptop and turned off my phone. I filled in my mom and dad about every single thing I'd do after school and the exact time I'd be home, and then I bolted out the door. I tried not to think about what they would do to me once they read the blog.

• • •

Mike was standing at my locker, without the harem or the jocks. All six-foot-four of him, smiling with his Colgate-commercial charm. And damn if he wasn't in his football jersey. Oh, God. Be. Cool.

"Hey, I saw your new post this morning. Pretty great stuff, Coretta."

"Oh, yeah, thanks." I couldn't really understand why he was bringing this up, at a time when it seemed like he might break up with me. Trying to soften the blow?

"Now listen, I sent it to my parents, and they were really impressed."

I had no idea how to respond, so I just smiled. What is it with people and sending things to their parents? Besides, Mike's parents were something altogether different, even from the Bernsteins. Long story short: Douglas and Esther Cornelius are very prominent African-American venture capitalists. (The few, the proud.) When I go to their house, I feel like I shouldn't stare at anything too long, because it's all so expensive and fragile. My eyes aren't rich enough for it.

"Mike, I didn't write that thinking your parents would see it, and I don't think that—"

He put his finger on my mouth.

I believe the term is "shushing." Yes, he shushed me. It was the first time he'd ever done that.

"Coretta, before you start, they sent it to all of their business and media contacts. You, my dear, are becoming quite the sensation."

Buzz. A text from Rachel.

Ummm. You have 7,000 followers! WHAT!?

I'm not sure exactly what my face looked like, but it felt like my eyes were bulging out of my head and might fall out onto the floor.

Seven thousand followers? How is this possible?

CHAPTER THREE

Karl (November 20, 2014)

Coretta White had far more than seven thousand followers by the time she crossed my radar, of course. When Alex's call came, she had over 700,000.

She was also realer than anyone I'd ghosted for in a long time.

After accepting the job and placing R$$P back on my communications table, I leaned back on the Big Silver Ball into a gentle back-bend, then closed my eyes and lingered on thoughts of my ex-girlfriend-turned-employer. I was careful not to fall on my head. In the six months I'd been sitting on the BSB, I had fallen on my head exactly twice. Still, I could really feel the difference in my core strength.

Unfortunately my six-pack was still obscured by the countless other six-packs that had passed through over the decades. Ice Cream and Beer: the Two Pillars of My Visible Prosperity, the foundation of my formidable paunch.

Reflecting on my twenty-year relationship with Alex was akin to visiting an absurd carnival fun house populated with the rich and powerful. Strobe-lit pockets revealed glimpses of autistic Nobel Prize winners, plastic-smile politicians, menopausal titans of industry. From unseen passageways sprang gum-popping teenybopper stars, lascivious celebrity chefs, and rappers who ranged from the monosyllabic coma-toast to wide-eyed megalomaniacs.

I shared the price of admission with a secret cadre of misfit friends and occasional subcontractors when the workload got too heavy.

Alex was aware of all of them and was always there along with us—but somehow removed, above it all, *herself*.

Now the prospect of fostering a single identity—the truly amazing Coretta White—had an unsettling result. It made me question my own identity. I tried to rewind, so I could make some sense of the endless stream of someone elses I had inhabited. Half of my life, it occurred to me, had been devoted to pretend time, to imagining myself as someone other than Karl Ristoff.

For the first time ever, for the first time since Alex had brought me into this ghost-racket, I actually found myself wondering about my "true self."

Who was I? *What* was I?

I saw no point in apprising Alex of my plunge into uncertainty.

Back in college I'd based my identity around being in a band, the Peter O'Toole Society*. We were a campus sensation, drawing crowds in small Cambridge clubs, getting paid to play parties and school-sanctioned trip-fests at colleges throughout the Northeast.

Possessing no discernable musical ability but plenty of unrestrained personality, I was the front man. An early '90s white rapper convinced that I was the heir apparent to the Beastie Boys*. The rest of the group was essentially a proto-typical four-piece Ivy League jam band—drums, guitar, bass, and keys—and they were frighteningly good. Too good for me, it turned out, although I'm not sure why it took them three years to realize it.

Exactly one week after we landed ourselves in *Rolling Stone* magazine as one of the "Best College Bands in the USA," I was fired. Our guitarist broke the news. He and the other three members of the Peter O'Toole Society wanted to break up so they could embark on "a new project." This new project would consist of the original band minus me. Apparently they were being held back creatively by having to play "behind a white rapper."

I didn't see the point of arguing my case. If they wanted to swap showmanship and charisma for the creative freedom to take mushrooms and play extended interpolations of The Meters'* greatest hits, well, that was their pickle, and they could suck it.

On the other hand, Alex first met me at a POTS show. She made it abundantly clear that she was interested in me *in spite of* my stage persona, M.C. Expensive Meal aka Dick Johnson.

"Please stop rapping," she pleaded, about two months into our relationship. "Just . . . don't rap. Okay?"

"But rap is in my blood, baby."

In retrospect I find it hard to believe that I made such a pronouncement without irony. "Rap is in my blood, baby"? I must have been saying that as a joke, right? But my memory is of a perfectly straight-faced (and much thinner) younger self articulating those exact words, and Alex staring back with a look of abject pity. There was enough pity for both of us.

"No. It's not. It's not in your blood, Karl. It's in your penis." She affectionately mussed my curly high-top fade. "And in some other tiny, very stupid portion of your brain."

She was right. I was twenty-two years old. I had a diploma

from Harvard. It was time to give up my dreams of rap stardom.

Alex drew me close. "Karl, there are so many other ways you can make a living—and a real life for yourself—using your mind and your gift with words. You *are* a wordsmith. But if you do decide to keep rapping, well, I don't want to hear about it."

We broke up three weeks later. Not because Alex told me I'd never make it as a rapper.

On second thought, that's probably exactly why we broke up. Thankfully, Alex coerced me into our lifetime-guaranteed friendship pact.

Three weeks after that, she called to offer me my first gig working for her new company.

AllYou™ is a rare example of genius. In an age where "genius" is tossed around like glitter and bestowed upon the likes of Lady Gaga, the word has lost the weight it deserves. But at the age of twenty-two, Alex Melrose conceived of a comprehensive concierge service to provide "that one perfect person" to fulfill the individual needs of the super rich. She did this in the middle of a recession. And she started the company with nothing more than a Rolodex (if you don't know what a Rolodex is, Google it, kids), at her desk in the humongous Chelsea loft her art-dealer parents bought her as soon as she received her MBA.

Believe it or not, the western edge of Chelsea was a sketchy neighborhood back then. To me, it felt like a risky place to open a boutique business geared toward the top point-one percent (that's *point*-one percent).

Now the property is worth ten times what they paid for it.

Alex, like her parents, has always operated ahead of the

curve. Even then, she had that uncanny art-dealer talent for bringing the right people together at the right time. She explained to me that when it came to the promise of luxury goods and services, the extremely wealthy were immune to redundancy and hyperbole.

That's where I came in. I was her first "highly specialized specialist."

Based on a PowerPoint presentation I'd helped her create for one of her cutthroat business school classes, Alex decided I was the one perfect person to assist the Deputy US Commerce Secretary.

Madame Deputy happened to be the wife of one of Alex's pointedly powerful professors. She was computer illiterate but too embarrassed to admit as much to her employed assistants. As she made clear to AllYou™ (Alex and her Rolodex), she desperately needed help presenting her report on money laundering and transnational crime at the twentieth G7 summit in Italy.

My highly specialized specialty: I knew how to use PowerPoint.

Remember, this was 1994, a time when very few people realized how easy (or lame) it was to use Office Suite for Microsoft Word in general. The best part about the gig was that I got to travel to Naples and spend an afternoon in the same room as three prime ministers, four presidents, and a chancellor. Oh, and I got paid five thousand dollars. Not bad for my first week of honest work as a college graduate. Alex was thrilled.

Other high-profile PowerPoint gigs followed. I developed a knack for distilling big ideas into digestible bits of content, easily consumed by a broad range of participants in a group setting. In some ways Twitter is a lot like PowerPoint—a natural vehicle for disseminating self-promotional bullshit—but I'm getting ahead of myself.

As the twentieth century wound down, I created PowerPoint presentations for some of the greatest minds in economics, public policy, and reinsurance*. Their brainpower was best spent elsewhere, at least according to their own worshipful views of themselves. Meanwhile, I was traveling the world, staying in five-star hotels, always as an anonymous "assistant."

I knew it couldn't last forever, but why hit the brakes? I didn't even mind the Brooks Brothers suits and black wingtips, the "respectable work clothes" Alex insisted on buying for me.

A few of the smarter CEOs and politicians tried to woo me away from Alex, but she would never let such a thing happen. Not that she wanted to hold onto *me* specifically, but Alex understood that if *any* of her "specialists" were to be poached by one of her clients, her healthy commissions would disappear. From day one, all of her contracts—with clients as well as specialists—contained ironclad non-compete and nondisclosure clauses. And all payments, naturally, went through AllYou™. I'd go to jail before I'd get another job.

My PowerPoint career peaked when Alex agreed to loan my exclusive services for a three-month period—during which a certain high-powered, right-wing female CEO plotted a run for US Congress. This woman was so impressed with my PowerPoint acumen that she wanted to hire me as her head speechwriter.

She lost the election (through no fault of my own; no speech can undo the damage of a husband's indictment for insider trading), but she loved my speeches so much that she negotiated an extended deal with Alex for me to ghostwrite her memoir.

It turned out to be a *New York Times* bestseller.

Even though my name appeared nowhere in the pages of the book or any related materials, Alex made sure word got around about AllYou™'s prowess for finding that "one perfect ghostwriter." For some reason, most of Alex's politician clients ended up falling on the right side of the political spectrum. I soon found myself working on speeches for people I reviled. But I never let my personal worldview get in the way of making a buck.

In 1999 I helped write autobiographies for three of the five female Fortune 500 CEOs, and for two of the ten women who served in the US Senate—all at the same time.

If you think ghostwriting five books in one year is a lot, you're right. It is. On the other hand, five female CEOs out of five hundred? That's a poor statistic. But as of 2013, there are twenty-one female Fortune 500 CEOs and twenty women serving in the US Senate. That's progress!

Maybe I should be thanked? If so, you're welcome.

But ghostwriting isn't really writing. It's more like translating. The ghostwriter does not make things up. A ghostwriter must convince the reader that his words have emanated from an attributed author's brain. But more importantly, he must compose the author's story in a way that is compelling to the reader.

Then there is the delicate relationship between ghostwriter and "author." A skilled ghostwriter will never allow the author to feel that his or her own stories are being rewritten because they are otherwise un-fucking-readable. Rather, the ghostwriter is merely "helping bring the author's own words to life on the page."

Okay, five books in one year *was* too much. I shouldn't complain, since I made a shit-ton of money. But when the last inspirational tale of bootstraps-to-Burberry was in the can, I was completely fed up with skirt-suits, skinny lattes, and private drivers. I was also convinced that the "book" as we knew it was an endangered species, but that it might very well outlive the magazine. That made me anxious. If I wasn't a rapper, at least I was a writer, a wordsmith. Wasn't I?

When I was in college, my weed dealer Clarence gave me some important advice. (Full Disclosure: I have not smoked weed with any regularity for more than fifteen years, and since the year 2000 I have been virtually drug free, except for alcohol, coffee, cigarettes, and Adderall.) He took a huge bong hit and began speaking in that tight-lipped, constricted voice that precedes the exhalation. "My biggest regret about getting into the business"—here he enveloped me in a cloud of pungent smoke—"is not giving myself a pseudonym. I should have told all my custies my name was Jay, like every other Tom, Dick, and Larry who sells weed. And now look at me. I'm Clarence the Weed Guy. Not Clarence the DJ. Not Clarence with the Amazing Record Collection. Not Clarence Who Makes the Killer Gazpacho. Just Clarence the Weed Guy."

I was too stoned to follow. "Custies?" I asked. "What's that?"

"Customers."

"Is that what I am, a custie?"

"Yeah, kid, you're a custie." He loaded the bong and passed it to me with a sad smile. "Listen, if you ever find yourself doing something that you don't want to be known for doing—especially if it's something you're doing purely for money, or if it's illegal or unethical in any way—I strongly advise you to adopt a pseudonym. An alias. An aka. In life, we are never required to tell the truth."

AM I BORING YOU, DEAR READER?

Please forgive this prolonged section of overwrought personal business history! I'm just trying to get to the part where I became an Internet soothsayer.

Years before I happened upon Coretta White and *Little White Lies*, I proved to Alex Melrose that I, too, could be ahead of the curve. Which helps elucidate why my friend and employer believed that I was the Magical White Man qualified to help this Rich Little Black Girl write a blog—specifically a blog that did *not* require a ghostwriter.

It's hard to fathom that from 2002 to 2005, blogs ruled. And I ruled the blogs. Some of them, at any rate. During that time, I must have blown through hundreds of thousands of dollars made on blogs alone. Some content I wrote myself, or rather rewrote for the so-called "blogger." On some blogs I was more of an editor, farming out writing assignments to a tiny, trusted army of minions.

I didn't bother Alex with putting my subcontractors on the books, or frankly mentioning them to her at all. My fees from AllYou™ were direct-deposited to my bank account, and I paid all my workers in cash, under the table. Cash goes fast in New York City, after all. With all the fine restaurants, overpriced cocktails, and cab fares, it's hard to keep money in the bank.

But somehow Alex knew about my minions. Alex always knew everything.

Fortunately, AllYou™ also deducted my taxes before direct-depositing. My tax returns were generously prepared by Alex's in-house accountant. Most years I signed the returns without even reading the dollar amounts. There was nothing left in my bank account, so why bother knowing how much I had made in the first place? I was king of the ghost-blogs. That was all that mattered.

At least until the 2005 AllYou™ holiday party. Then everything changed.

Since 1996 Alex had hosted this annual AllYou™ holiday bacchanal (she called it a Christmas party until 2000) at that same Chelsea loft where she'd started. She lavished gifts upon all those who benefited from her genius—*her* tiny and trusted army of minions, of which I was Minion Number One. All of us were sworn to the same rigid code of anonymity and secrecy, which of course led to lots of drinking.

It was here, less than three months after Facebook launched, that I made the audacious prediction it would take over the World Wide Web.

Back then Facebook was still intended for high school and college kids. I swore that it would make Friendster and Myspace and maybe even Google obsolete.

God, I love eggnog.

One year later, having been proved at least partly right, I learned Alex decided I should (anonymously and secretly) head up the new social networking division of AllYou™. The money was good, and the work was easy. The problem was that I no longer met interesting and powerful people. Facebook was all about corporations. I got stuck coaching a bunch of clueless marketing directors. Herders of sheeple. And I was their schlepherd.

My hate for all things corporate was starting to give me back pain. And I missed writing. Maybe even more than I missed rapping.

Then came Twitter.

• • •

At the 2007 holiday party, I found myself preaching to Alex about the amazing potential of "a new microblogging and social networking site." (God, I *do* love eggnog.) I hypocritically quoted Twitter's corporate words because in this instance, I believed them. I could see the cash written all over the cow.

And per my prediction, when Twitter emerged as the preferred medium for fame seekers, it was like God's gift to me. I became its secret weapon. I was indeed #KingTwit, Dark Lord of the Twitterverse.

I became increasingly convinced of my *own* genius as well.

So four years later, I was eggnog-fueled enough to announce that I would not be accepting any more corporations as clients. I got in this business to help Alex's *people*. Like that first poor client who didn't know how to create a PowerPoint presentation. And I did not believe corporations were people.

"Well, neither do I," Alex offered in rebuttal, helping herself to another sloppy ladleful. "But their money is quite green. As green as a person's, and often comes in larger sums."

Now here I was on the BSB wondering if it would ever occur to Alex that I might *not* be motivated by money.

Maybe she would never realize that my motivation stemmed from unwavering loyalty to her. (Maybe that was best.) Loyalty, and the love of a challenge, and a fierce pride in my ability to write convincingly and on demand. On some level, it stemmed from a belief in my own genius.

On the other hand, Alex knew me better than anyone else. She'd offered me the Coretta White gig for a reason. She knew I was ready for a break. Twitter may have been my bitch once, but I was now a prisoner of the Twittersphere. I was Twitter's bitch. I was twizzered. Tweeked. Tweezled.

"You know I love the color green, Alex," I'd told her at the end of today's fateful phone call. "But in my heart, I'm a wordsmith."

CHAPTER FOUR

Coretta (September 25–November 18, 2013)

tumblr.

LITTLE WHITE LIES

September 25, 2013

Little White Lie of the Day: "Free your ass, and your mind will follow." Translation: "Young women, you need to keep up with the Kardashians (or the Joneses) to stay relevant, current, and/or accepted." Also: this lie wasn't one my parents told me, but rather one that I told myself.

Anyone born from the early 1980s until the early 2000s is part of Gen Y or a "millennial." I'll accept the "millennial" label for the purpose of this post. As a millennial, I feel fortunate for all of the access I have been granted to information. I will never know the annoyance my parents idiotically suffer when sitting around with friends and trying to think of an actor's name from . . . wait, what's that film again? My friends and I know how to find Charlize Theron's shoe size. Instantly. That's progress.

We are so lucky. We have tools galore to keep us up to date. And so we have the burden of over-access like no generation before us. Obsession is as old as humanity itself. But in the fairly recent past, it used to be that if a girl was obsessed with Charlize Theron—or say, Marilyn Monroe—with that glamour, that beauty, that talent (?), yadda yadda, she would read a magazine article, go watch a movie of hers, and I don't know . . . just be a fan.

So let's look at the Kardashians, shall we? They've been exalted to Tudor status in that they're a family name that's a Snapchat of their entire civilization. And like the Tudors, they haven't contributed anything to that civilization. They aren't even particularly controversial. (No drug use, Lamar Odom excluded.) Kim put out a sex tape that made her famous because we saw her butt "by accident." I did not watch the tape, but I still say "we," because I participate in the same lie. We continue to be obsessed even though we all know she used her own butt to launch herself as a celebrity.

"Free your mind, and your ass will follow," as a great black revolutionary once said. Google it, Mom and Dad, in case you don't remember. It was George Clinton.

Kim Kardashian has shown us the Millennial Truth, which is the opposite: "Free your ass, and your mind will follow."

Need proof? All of the other Kardashians soon became famous on the tail of Kim's butt.

So why am I a part of this? That's where the horror lies. I am guilty. WHY DO I FEEL THE NEED TO FOLLOW KHLOE ON INSTAGRAM? She/they are uploading pictures of Lamborghinis, $10,000 handbags, and pictures the paparazzi took of them . . . that they somehow saved and uploaded to their own accounts? Why do I know so much about Bruce Jenner's plastic surgery horrors? Or Bruce and Kris Jenner's sex life? Or that Rob can't control his weight or his OCD? Or Khloe and Lamar's divorce? Why do I know that Scott is a pain in the @$$ of a human? I

don't know . . . but I guess I read it? Saw it on TV? Who is the
Secretary General of the UN? I don't know!

Now I do. FYI, it's Ban ki-Moon.

My mom knows about the Kardashian women because
she secretly shares my obsession. It's not just millennials. So
tomorrow, why can't we sit around the breakfast table looking
to women—hell, even celebrities—who are actually saying
something that means something? You're young once, I get it.
It's not bad to be entertained by the circus from time to time.

I may know that Charlize Theron wears a 9.5 shoe, but hey,
she also has an HIV outreach charity in South Africa. Let's stop
Keeping Up with the Kardashians and, I don't know, Keep Up
with the Clintons? Maybe not George, but Hillary? Can we
make them a Snapchat of our civilization? Okay, maaaaybe
minus a few years in the White House for Bill, but you get the
gist . . .

My prayers to become a morning person went unanswered.

I'd been inspired to write a post last night for reasons I
couldn't remember now. At least my parents were smiling
from behind their respective iPad and newspaper. I stared
into my cereal bowl for what could have been three days or
three seconds. I grabbed my phone just to remind myself that
I was actually awake and not in a dream state. I made my
rounds on social media. Facebook, Twitter, Tumblrrrrrrrrr—
WHAT?! *Little White Lies* had 30,027 followers—wait,
30,157—wait, 30,200 . . .

As I was watching the number of followers climb, my
mother was watching the cereal pour out of my mouth. She
stopped smiling. "Coretta, that's not cute."

"I, ummm . . . yeah, sorry. Mornings, huh?"

My father folded his newspaper and set it down. "You

wouldn't be salivating over the amount of new followers you got overnight, would you?" he asked gently.

"Oh, no. I just love rice-based cereal products, you know—"

"Coretta, honey, stop." My dad put his hand on my shoulder, which could only mean something really good, or something really bad. "You don't have to hide your successes from us. We are very proud of you and of this blog. You never told us you were such a great writer."

I wanted to say that I never told them because I never *knew* I was such a great writer. I once wrote a short story in eighth grade. I was supremely pleased with it. When I read it to my parents, they asked me why it didn't have an ending. They weren't being facetious. Until now, that had defined my writing career.

"Oh, you guys, thanks. Yeah, it's nothing, I mean it's something, but thanks." Call me a Kardashian; I managed to say nothing while using all those words.

My mother was smiling again. "Well, colleges are going to be taking notice, Coretta. It seems you're on your way to becoming a voice of your generation, whether you like it or not. You keep doing you, and be proud of that."

Now I was worried. My mother was given to overstatement and ridiculousness; that was the whole point of the blog. But not when it came to *me*. Since when did she use the phrases "voice of a generation" or "you keep doing you"? I ran out of the house even faster than the last time I'd posted.

This morning couldn't get any weirder—right?

Don't worry, dear reader. That's a rhetorical question.

As I walked up to school I noticed that a lot of the kids were smiling at me the way Mom and Dad had.

Let's get one thing straight: I'd been the center of attention plenty of times. I admit that I've suffered from delusions of grandeur. But this was different. People really *were* looking at me differently. I made sure I hadn't forgotten a major article of clothing. Pants, shirt, shoes—okay, I was covered. But once again, I felt like I was in a teen movie. This time it wasn't so much a Tyler Perry teen movie as much as a generic *I was in the montage where everyone looks at the girl in a different way* . . . and as embarrassment consumes her and she makes her way to her locker, *BAM!* There is her knight in shining armor (letterman's jacket), ready to whisk her away to homeroom.

Mike grinned from one perfectly symmetrical ear to the other. He walked right up to me and kissed me. Like, *kissed* me. Again with the PDA. His hand was on the back of my head; the other was on the small of my back. This was not Mike, and this was especially not Mike in school.

"What's going on?" I asked point-blank, once I could get ahold of myself.

"Coretta, I read your Tumblr this morning. Correction: my parents and I read your post. They are so impressed by you, which is saying a lot."

I tried to smile back, but couldn't. *Here we go with the parents again.* What was his and Rachel's problem? Out of the corner of my eye I saw Ms. Schuster, my AP English teacher, walking straight for us. Speaking of grown-ups, here came one who was about to lecture us on Mike's use of his tongue to check my tonsils for strep.

Of course it had to be Ms. Schuster, who hated PDA more than the average teacher. Rumor had it that she'd never had a single human relationship in her entire life. On her desk there was a framed 8x10 portrait-studio photo of her with three

German shepherds in choke collars. The dogs, not her, but still, she was wearing a turtleneck—both in the picture and right now. She always wore turtlenecks, as far as I could tell.

She didn't look angry, though. In fact, she beamed at me.

"Ms. White, I've been reading your blog," she said as Mike backed away from me. "Very interesting commentary. If it's all right with you, I'd like to include *Little White Lies* as part of my creative writing exercises next week."

"Creative writing. Yes, uhhh, yes, okay, do as you see justice to your course . . . Ms. Schuster."

So those words did not come out as planned, but they were enough to get her to nod and walk away.

Can we all please process that she knew the name of my blog? I'd been publicly befriended by the Booker T. Washington High School equivalent of Professor Snape from *Harry Potter*.

"Wow, looks like you're making friends with the enemy," Mike mused, enjoying himself.

Before I could respond, Rachel appeared. The morning kept getting better.

"The enemy? Who is friends with the enemy? Wait, who is the enemy? Is it me? No, it's not me. Never mind. Hi! Good morning, superstar!"

I leaned against my locker, exhausted. "Hey, girl. Mike's just talking about Ms. Schuster."

"Oh, right. Well, I wanted to see what time you wanted to meet tonight to work on the plan for the Spanish club party. It's the first party of the year, and you know how I feel about first impressions. I have a storyboard already outlined."

Shit. My stomach dropped. I slapped my forehead. "Oh, gosh, Rachel, I'm sorry. I totally forgot. I have two papers due tomorrow that I haven't even started—"

"Ha, ha, very funny."

I shook my head. "I'm not joking."

Rachel's smile grew strained. She shot a quick glance at Mike. "But Coretta, you're the president. You *have* to be at the party-planning meeting. I can't be in charge of all of this."

"No, I know, I know. Let me ask Jessica if she can help out—"

"Jessica doesn't even know how to conjugate the infinitive of a verb," Rachel interrupted.

I wasn't sure what to say. Rachel took cancellations very personally. Two years ago, I had to cancel a Saturday afternoon plan to make friendship bracelets. We were on the phone for eighty-seven minutes on Sunday to smooth things out. I always try to keep my plans with her because it really isn't worth the cell-phone minutes not to. That being said, I couldn't afford the setback of not turning in two papers on time.

"Rachel, I'm really sorry. I'll make it up to you, I promise."

By now Mike was staring at the floor. His smile was long gone.

Rachel shrugged. "Forget it. Have fun writing your papers."

I went through that day feeling like a jerk about Rachel. And feeling excited that my Tumblr was becoming a sensation of sorts. And feeling appreciated by Mike—more than ever, actually. And feeling proud that my parents were so impressed with me.

I was feeling a lot of weird and contradictory things.

But in the end, the feeling that took over was impending doom. I had way too many commitments piling up.

Whatever. Don't think about it. It'll all get done. It always does. I stayed up all night and finished those papers.

• • •

Two weeks had passed since my sort-of fight with Rachel, and I hadn't slowed down. I'd done the opposite: I'd put up a LWL post every night. I kept telling myself that I wasn't going to post *every* night, that I was going to focus on my college applications, or hang out with Mike, or show up at Rachel's and apologize in person . . . but something inevitably came up. Some issue, some celebrity, some political injustice—hell, even some newfound beauty tip—all of it made me jump to my computer.

Tonight would be different. No blogging.

I'd vowed to start on my first personal essay for Howard University. It was Friday. I was missing Mike's home football game, which I could justify. I was staying home to further my academic future. (Besides, when was the last time you heard of an NFL wide receiver from Brooklyn?) But then . . . *Oh, look at that, someone sent me a message on my blog.*

I could read a message. That wasn't *writing* a post; that was reading a message, and that was allowed. I'd been getting messages from random readers—mainly just encouraging words, and the occasional disturbing sexual weirdness, which I reported. I opened it up, expecting one or the other.

October 7, 2013

Hi, Coretta,

 My name is Becca, and I've been reading your blog since your very first post. You are such an inspiration to me and to so many teenagers reading *Little White Lies*. I'm writing you because I really don't know who else to turn to. I'm afraid that if I

tell my parents, friends, or anyone at school that I'll start a storm
that I won't be able to stop. So here it goes . . .

I'm a sophomore in high school, and to put it frankly, I'm
bullied. I'm bullied so much that I feel like I can't take it anymore. I
don't even really know what that means, but I know that I'm at my
breaking point. I know that I'm never going to be pretty enough,
or smart enough, or popular enough for these kids. And the worst
part is, I agree with most of the things that they say about me.

I guess, what I'm asking you is, what would you do if you
were me?

Please help.

Becca

What? *What?!* My stomach sank as I read each word. Why
did Becca think that I was the one she should confide in?

*I'm only seventeen years old. I still wash all my clothes in
one load. Becca, I don't sort my colors!* I took a deep breath and
repeated my new mantra: *Stay calm. Stay calm.* It didn't help.

I needed to write her back. I couldn't just send this one
to the trash. *I* was bullied, after all (Coretta Cock-Ring,
anyone?), but once I'd made it out of the nightmare that
was middle school—and gotten my headgear removed—it all
worked itself out. Becca needed to know that. Howard University could wait.

October 7, 2013

Dear Becca,

Thank you for messaging me. It really means a lot that you
reached out. I know that feeling of thinking you're not good enough,
or smart enough, or pretty enough, or just enough. While I don't
know you personally, Becca, I already know that you're enough.

People tear down other people as a way to make themselves feel better. It seems cliché, and maybe it is, but it's also true.

Every one of those kids at school that is bullying you is using your pain as a way to mask whatever insecurities they have. You can't do anything about their insecurities. The only thing you can do is take care of yourself, and the best way to do that is to reach out to people and resources around you that can help.

You asked me what I would do, and here it is:

1.   Tell your parents. They need know, Becca, trust me.
2.   Visit this website: http://www.stopbullying.gov/get-help-now/index.html.
     It has resources for kids that are looking for help. They know what to do and can help you and your parents navigate the school system chain.
3.   Reach out to your school officials (with your parents or an adult you trust), as you'll see on that website. You're not doing this just for yourself, but you're doing it to take a stand for the others who feel lost and beat down.
4.   Please let me know if any of this is confusing, or if you need anything else.

Thank you again for reaching out. Please be safe, and take these steps immediately, because you shouldn't have to spend another day not feeling like you're enough.

With love,
Coretta White

A few days later, I found out that Becca did take my advice. She received the help she needed. I also doubt that she will ever be bullied again—because the way I found out was on a local news segment.

On television.

The word was out: *Coretta White will give you personal advice.* After that, my inbox was flooded. Hundreds of deeply troubled people of all ages reached out. A forty-seven-year-old (presumably) white male from Indiana asked me whether he should surprise his wife with NASCAR tickets for their anniversary. Ummmm . . . ask the group of middle-aged (presumably) white men who are your friends? A fourteen-year-old girl asked me if she should get an IUD or low-dose estrogen birth control pills. Ummm . . . ask a gynecologist? A person asked if they should get rid of their dog because of its aggression or try to retrain it. Ummmm . . . ask Cesar the Dog Whisperer?

Saturday I got a text from Mike. He forgave me for missing the game. Ah, my sweet Mike. Also, his parents wanted to have me over for dinner. When I read that, I began to sweat.

I spent two hours picking out a dress that I felt was worthy of their home. I practiced looking at expensive things in magazines and not acting flabbergasted.

Dinner was great, but an anxious blur, as expected. Now we were all just sitting at the table, lingering over dessert, and I couldn't help but feel like something was up.

Mike's mother, Esther, broke the silence. "Coretta, I'm sure Mike has been updating you, but both Douglas and I have been very entertained by your Tumblr."

She reminded me of someone, and I just couldn't place it . . .

Mike's dad chimed in as if this was planned. "Yes, we've been talking about it quite a bit lately."

It was Claire Huxtable. She reminded me of Bill Cosby's TV wife, updated from the 1980s to 2013. High cheekbones, eyes that had seen a thousand lifetimes, graceful but could easily put someone in their place with a bat of her eyelashes.

If I tried to put someone in their place with my eyelashes, people would ask if I was having a seizure.

"Thank you so much." What else was I supposed to say? Mike was just sitting there. I felt like he was supposed to chime in with a deflection.

Come on, Mike, I silently pleaded. *Step up.*

Mrs. Cornelius smirked. "Coretta, I know you and Michael spend quite a bit of time volunteering at SKOOLS 4 ALL. How would you say that is going?"

Oh my God, this is how I die: embarrassment. My boyfriend's mother knows we make out under the guise of helping children. "Umm, I like it?"

"I know it must be a lot for you to volunteer for so many hours after school in addition to keeping up with your schoolwork and extracurricular activities."

Was this entrapment? I decided to play stupid by playing smart. "You know, it does seem like a lot on paper, but it all just seems to work." A cheese-eating grin sprang across my face, like I'd just won the blue ribbon at the county fair.

Esther looked at Douglas, and he nodded back at her. "Coretta, I want to cut to the chase—Douglas and I are on the board at Pulse TV, and we talked to them about you. They are very interested in your blog."

Of course I knew that they were on the board of Pulse TV. It was how I'd hooked up with—er, "met"—their son in the first place. Esther and Cornelius were there at that very first SKOOLS 4 ALL fundraiser over the summer. They'd seen Mike flirt with me. And they'd clearly approved. So the whole fake formality of this interrogation had now officially put me on edge. *Who* exactly was interested in my blog? Who were *they,* other than Mike's parents?

Finally Mike cleared his throat. "The Skool twins really

like the stance you took against bullying. They'd like to talk
to you about starting a TV show, babe. How cool is that?"

Ah, he *could* speak. How encouraging.

He was smiling. So was I. Like an idiot again, frankly. I'd
never thought about having my own TV show. Well, it's not
that I never thought about having my own TV show, it's that
I'd never thought it'd actually be possible. As cynical as I
wanted to be about it all, the idiotic smile wouldn't go away.
The Corneliuses weren't known for handing out false compliments—or compliments in general.

Mr. Cornelius took his final bite of key lime pie and peered
intently at me. He leaned his fork against the dessert plate.
"Coretta, would you be willing to meet with the Skool twins
if we were to set up the meeting?"

Despite my comment on how it all just seemed to work,
I wasn't exactly twiddling my thumbs in all my free time.
If I was twiddling my thumbs at all, it was because I was
trying to tread water with any part of my body that *had*
free time. "Let me talk to my parents," I said after a minute.

Mr. Cornelius nodded knowingly. "Very wise. And Coretta,
I'm sure Karin and Anders would understand if you needed
to back off on your volunteer time at SKOOLS 4 ALL, should
it become too much on paper."

We all laughed together. But I alone secretly cringed, for
myriad reasons.

In the two weeks that followed my fancy dinner at Mike's
house, I'd:

1. Half-assed a Spanish club meeting but ordered Taco
   Bell for the group so nobody would complain.
2. Participated in a law club mock trial wherein my client
   was found guilty because I wrote a LWL rant on cat

people the night before. Seriously, though, what is it with people and cats? Sick.

3. Let Rachel go thrifting alone, which meant I was punished by sheer guilt every time I saw a pre-owned piece of clothing that never should have been bought the first time.

4. Stopped volunteering at SKOOLS 4 ALL. Three hours of sleep a night apparently does not provide the best mental state for nonprofit work.

My interactions with Mike were centered on text messages that usually revolved around Pulse TV, and my attempts to avoid answering. I didn't want anyone to know why I was debating if I could handle the time commitment. I had hopes that I would pull myself up by my bootstraps, and that a master plan would hit me when the time was right. My GPA, which was once a proud 4.0 (yes, that is *perfect*), had dropped to a 3.7. That might not seem like a big deal, but I assure you, for the schools that my parents expected me to go to, that was a very big deal.

I kept going back and forth on meeting with Pulse TV. Of course I wanted to have my own TV show, but I preferred not to become a high school dropout in the process. Obligations were really starting to pile up. I was waiting for the clock to strike master plan o'clock.

My phone buzzed again. It was Mike.

> Babe, have you decided if ur going to meet with the Skool twins yet? They want to meet w/ u jan 3rd. My parents were asking . . .

No, I hadn't decided, which is why I hadn't responded.

Little White Lies had become a monster of its own. I was writing at least three posts a week, not to mention responding to the personal messages that left me wondering if someone might take their own lives if I didn't. Every time I looked in the mirror, I expected all my hair to have fallen out. I should have been bald from stress. The universe had been kind enough to let me keep it for now. That was the only upside, that one day I could finally start to grow my Afro.

Thanksgiving break was fast approaching, at least. Maybe I'd have time to catch up on all of my schoolwork and do some extra credit to pull up that GPA before my parents or any colleges noticed.

I looked at Mike's text message one more time. Then I thought about it. Colleges would be really impressed by a seventeen-year-old with a 3.7 GPA *and* a TV show. Why hadn't this all made sense to me before? I needed this show. I could make it work; I always did.

> Yes, I'll do it. Jan 3.

Is it a good sign that upon hitting SEND I immediately wanted to barf? I chose to believe that yes, it was. A text came in almost immediately—Rachel.

> It's set: Jan. 3rd is the student council regional meeting. Since we are the home school, we will be in charge of coordinating the accommodations for the visiting schools. Let's meet tomorrow?

Rachel has the most properly punctuated texts of anyone I know. But . . . WAIT! WHAT? JANUARY THIRD? Was I into self-sabotage? I had just canceled on Rachel six times in a row. Every day at school I was surprised to see that her head had not yet exploded. I had to meet her tomorrow. I had to.

Oh, great, another text. This one was from Mike.

> Jan 3rd at 4PM, set in stone! So excited for you!

Set in stone. That's funny, that's exactly how I was feeling at that very moment. Okay, this was fine, this was *fine*, THIS was FINE. Nobody has ever died from a blog, right? This sounds like a question someone would ask me. To which I'd answer, "Let's wait and see."

Rachel and I met at her house after school to talk about this regional student council meeting. I felt like those people on *Celebrity Rehab with Dr. Drew*, minus the addiction. (Though maybe my addiction was *Little White Lies*.) I was so tired, so stressed out, so afraid that she was going to see through my routine of "I'm really doing great, guys!"

We were in her bedroom, which always felt like home. Not surprisingly, it was still decorated the same as it was ten years ago. She even had the same Muppet stuffed animals on the bed, Kermit and Miss Piggy. I admired that about Rachel, how she was never restless for change. If her only addictions were thrift store clothing and her stuffed animal collection, good for her.

"Coretta, are you listening to me?"

"Yes, yes, of course." I wasn't, though. I hadn't really heard what she had been saying for the last five minutes. At least I thought it was five.

"Okay, what is your deal?" Rachel snapped. "You think you can just treat me like this because I'm not as Internet

famous as you or whatever, and I get that. This meeting, however, has a purpose beyond our friendship. Which, honestly,
doesn't seem all that important to you anymore."

Those words I heard.

The worst part? She was right. I hadn't just been
neglecting our friendship; I'd gone days without talking to
her, which hadn't happened since we could form words. As
I was trying to figure out what version of "I'm sorry" I'd
offer, tears started pouring from my eyes. I am not using
the word *pour* lightly. I'm talking about the kind of crying
where the tears don't even hit your cheeks. They just drop
right to the floor. I managed to get some words out. They
weren't terribly coherent.

"Rachel . . . I can't. The blog, and my GPA, school, and
the twins, Skool, and the messages, NASCAR? *Why?* I . . . I
am so sorry."

I buried my head in my lap and cried into her Rainbow
Brite pillow.

When I finally looked up, Rachel was staring at me. She
backed away, her lips twisted in a look of horror or concern or both. To be fair, I hadn't been showing any signs of
a breakdown, until, well, the breakdown itself. "Coretta,
what's going on?" she whispered.

"I've gotten way in over my head with the blog, and
my grades are suffering, and . . . and . . . and I scheduled a
meeting during the student council regional meeting! I think
I'm actually losing my mind."

Rachel nodded. "Just breathe, okay, just breathe. Everything is going to be okay." She bit her lip and looked up
toward the ceiling. This meant she was thinking of a plan.
Normally this was a bad sign, but at this point, I was willing
to take any advice. After all, at *this* point, she was the only

one who knew my dark secret. And let's face it: I needed all the help I could get.

Finally she took a deep breath. "Listen, I know someone that can help you lighten your load. There's a person I know of through my parents who specializes in this. The thing is, you have to trust me. Do you trust me?"

"Who is it? What do I have to do?"

"Do you trust me?" she repeated.

"Of course I do!"

She sat beside me, looking straight into my watery eyes. "Here's the thing, you can't know who the person is, and you can't tell anyone about this. Nobody can know, Coretta. Not Mike, not your parents, not my parents."

Now I'm not exactly a detective, but coming from anyone else, this offer might be classified as "shady." But this was Rachel. And what the hell? If she had a shady side, great. *I* did. The more I thought about it, the more I realized I could use some shade from the blistering limelight that was frying my brain.

"Yes. Yes. I'll trust you. I'll do anything. Thank you, Rachel. Thank you."

With that, I lay my head on Rainbow Brite's face, avoiding the puddle of snot.

CHAPTER FIVE

Karl (November 26 and December 3, 2013)

"Alex, darling, you've barely touched your steak." I glanced down at the glorious slab of meat—blackened crispy on the outside, juicy pink on the inside, expertly sliced and glistening with melted butter. I aimed a look of concern at her. "Is anything okay?"

She rolled her eyes and pushed the platter closer to me. "Bad joke, Karl. I haven't eaten meat for nearly ten years. You know that."

"Yes, but in the twenty years that I've lived in Brooklyn," I replied with maybe too much smug satisfaction, "Peter Luger Steakhouse* is the one thing in Williamsburg that hasn't changed at all."

"I don't think this place has changed much since the late nineteenth century."

"Exactly. Since eighteen eighty-seven. Remember that cab ride we took through this neighborhood about ten years ago? I was pointing to all the different buildings and businesses and saying, 'Changed, unchanged, changed, changed, changed, unchanged—'"

"Yes, I do. After two minutes I got really annoyed and asked you to stop."

I stabbed a piece of meat with my fork. "I know. And you still want to get out of Brooklyn as fast as humanly possible. I don't blame you. But my point is *everything* in this moneyed-hipster mecca of excess has changed. Everything except Peter Luger Steakhouse."

With that, I finally got a smile. "And what's so wrong with change, Karl?"

"Nothing, I guess, if it amounts to progress," I admitted. "But there's a lot to be said for consistency. I mean, look around." I gestured at the crowd, packed into the overly bright wood-paneled room—more German beer hall than American steakhouse. The faces were as pink as the meat on their plates. "You've got to admit, I picked the perfect place to discuss our new client, right? I don't see too many teenagers eating here, and not one black person."

"Well, you're right about that," Alex said, her smile fading. She looked down at the oversized tomato and raw onion slices on her plate. "Anyway . . ."

"Anyway," I echoed. "Seriously. Noprah? Are you really not going to tell me who's bankrolling this thing? And is it really not Oprah? Because I've been racking my brain—and the Internet—and I haven't discovered any African-American media moguls who are women, who *own* their own network, who aren't Oprah. And you do know her network is actually called OWN, right?"

"Don't patronize me more than you already have, Karl. It's not Oprah."

"Well, that clears things up," I lied.

Alex signaled our crusty old waiter for another martini. I flashed him a casual peace sign, by which I meant, *Make it two*.

"So let's talk Coretta White." I punctuated her name with a dreamy sigh. "My hero."

"Oh, please," Alex snapped. "As if you have any heroes."

"I'm serious, Alex. This chick is legit. She's the real deal."

"I know."

"So why does she need me? I mean, us." I took another bite of steak. "I mean, our services," I added in Errol Flynn style.

Alex glanced toward the exit. "We've been over this. She's grappling with schoolwork, college applications, et cetera."

"What's the et cetera?"

Alex turned back to me, her eyes glittering. "Pulse TV wants to develop a Coretta White TV show with a robust web presence. Something that capitalizes on the live-tweeting everyone in the sweet-spot demographic does during the Oscars or an election or a football game or—"

"Pulse TV?" I interrupted. "Are you linked up with the Skool twins? They're, like, taking over the world right now. Will I get a piece of the TV show?"

I knew I wasn't getting a piece of the TV show, but I was irritated at the way Alex had snapped into pitch mode with me. Like I was one of her rich-mummy clients who needed to be sold on something.

"At this point, no." Alex accepted her fresh martini from our ancient waiter and took a long deliberate sip. "This is really meant as a temporary measure to get her through a rough period."

"Temporary?" I ignored my own fresh cocktail. "I thought you said this could turn into something long-term and exclusive. And lucrative."

"It could, Karl." Alex set down her drink. "The blog isn't going away. She's going to need it to drive the popularity of the new show. Once she finishes her negotiations with Pulse TV, I'll be able to renegotiate the terms of your contract."

"And what are those terms?" I wondered.

Alex laughed. In that brief instant, in the way she forgot herself except to cover her mouth from spewing martini, I caught a glimpse of the girl I knew from college. But then she was gone.

"Since when does Karl Ristoff concern himself with the terms of his contracts? Aren't you working on your next mixtape or something?" Alex ignored my reaction to her cheap shot and took another sip. "Don't you worry about the money. That'll start pouring in as soon as you complete your first blog post. But things are going to run a bit differently with this client. Rather than go through me, you will be dealing directly with Miss White. Like in your PowerPoint days. Remember those?"

"She's Miss White now?"

"Coretta White. Whatever. She's a kid, Karl."

I recognized that tone. Alex called me a kid, too. She was calling me one right now. "Okay, that's cool," I said. But I was lying. Strange, but for the first time ever—really, the first time since Alex and I had begun our arrangement—I felt anxious about a new client. I'd never felt this way before, not with any of the countless big shots, celebrities, or power brokers I had impersonated in the past. They were part of an elite I envied and resented and knew deep down I'd never become, or even mingle with. But this was different. This was interfacing with and passing myself off as a seventeen-year-old girl. One I respected (i.e., not Selena Gomez).

Alex polished off her second martini. "Great. I'm setting up a phone call between the two of you for early next week."

"Phone call? Why a phone call? Can't we just email?"

"I need her to be comfortable with you, Karl," Alex

explained. "This is a big deal for her. And I think it will help if she hears your voice."

"Isn't my writing enough?"

"What do you mean?"

"Don't you think I can adequately reassure her with the written word?" I asked flatly.

Alex rolled her eyes. "She wants to be sure that you're not some forty-year-old wigger who failed as a rapper yet still insists on steeping himself in black culture."

I dropped my fork on my plate. "Please do not use the W-word, Alex." I wasn't joking. "I hate that word. It's patently offensive, and white people should not be allowed to use it any more than they should the N-word. And if Coretta uses—"

"It was my choice of words," Alex interrupted with a sigh. "Coretta did not say 'wigger.' She probably wants to be sure you don't think you have the ability to write 'black' just because you've been listening to Lil Wayne* for the past ten years and you know who Killer Mike* is."

I glared at the woman I once thought I could love. There was no reason to remind her that I'd tweeted for Birdman*, and he'd practically raised Lil Wayne as his son; Alex was no doubt running through the same list in her mind, the list she'd helped facilitate.

"I think the real question is not whether I can write 'black' but whether or not I can write Coretta White," I said.

"I have apprised her of your bona fides," Alex answered, her voice back to the All-Business Boss Lady 2013 edition. "Now just take the call when she rings. And don't put her on speakerphone."

The following Tuesday afternoon, I sat at my communications table, bouncing gently on BSB. I anticipated the familiar sounds of Pink Floyd, and the toothy grin of Tony Robbins to appear on trusty R$$P.

Our phone appointment was for 3 P.M. sharp. At 3:04 the cash register chimed, and Tony's face lit up—his smile reflecting mine, yet considerably brighter.

Props for Coretta: I love it when people are a few minutes late for appointments. I've always interpreted the promptness of others as a personal affront. That being said, I make it a point to always be on time myself—no offense intended. Once the bass line kicked in, I pressed the green bar. "Hello?"

"Hello, is this Karl?" The voice was not young and fresh, or really anything close to what I'd been expecting. I detected a hint of weariness, a healthy dose of wariness. She sounded like Alex, minus about five years.

"Yes, is this Coretta?" I tried to convey the casual confidence likely endorsed by Tony Robbins. "I hope you don't mind speakerphone. My ears don't accommodate those little earbuds."

"Okayyy." Coretta drew out the second syllable. Then we got into it.

Note from Karl: In order to present this initial phone meeting, I will dispense with the tedious he said/she said of traditional prose narrative and its attendant adverbs and adjectives. For the sake of abbreviation, K will stand for Karl, and C will signify Coretta.

K: Anyway, I prefer speakerphone. To tell you the truth, I live in this basement apartment—it's not really a basement, it's only, like, two steps down from street level. It's actually really nice—but for whatever reason, I have the worst cell service. And I never liked talking on the phone to begin with.

C: It's okay. I don't mind the speakerphone. And I can hear you fine.

K: Is it cool if I call you Coretta? You can call me Karl if you want. Or if we're texting or emailing, you can call me K. Or really you don't have to call me anything at all. You'll know you're writing to me, and of course I'll know it's to me, and I'll know it's from you, so once we get this thing going, we really won't have to call each other anything, okay?

C: Okayyy.

K: So, Coretta, it's not often that I am put in direct contact with a client. But since that is our arrangement, I would like very much to take advantage of this rare opportunity to hear from you directly. What do you expect of me?

C: [silence]

K: Coretta?

C: You don't sound as black as I thought you would.

K: You do realize I'm not black, don't you? I mean, you knew that, right?

C: Honestly, it didn't really come up. I think I assumed you were white? But I still thought you might have, like, a blacker-sounding voice or something. Is that racist?

K: Black people can't be racist.

C: Yes, they can.

K: Let's not get too deep into that shit just yet, all right? I mean, unless you want to.

C: Okayyy.

K: You do realize that I am also a man, don't you?

C: Yes.

K: And how does that make you feel, Coretta?

C: Excuse me?

K: Um, that was sort of meant as a joke. I was trying to sound like a therapist. I doubt you're in therapy. Yet. You seem well-adjusted. But I'm sure you've seen that stuff on TV, and I imagine half your friends are in therapy, or will be before you know it. Anyway, dumb joke, but I guess the question still stands: How *do* you feel about hiring a middle-aged white man to help you write your blog? And as long as we're at it, here's the follow-up question—

C: Whoa, hold on.

K: Sorry. I tend to ramble. On the phone. Which is why I hate it. Not in my work, of course.

C: Do you *not* want this job, Karl?

K: I just can't help wondering why you think you need me. You appear to be doing just fine on your own. Winning, in fact. Better than just about anyone out there. *Little White Lies* is a thing of beauty. Your voice is pitch-perfect. Your followers are engaged and adoring. I mean, sure, I could help you out with a few organizational things—just some formatting shit, really. This is, like . . . Kanye territory for me. You're someone special, Coretta. That sounded completely corny the way that came out, but it's true. And by the way, I think your Kanye coverage has been as cogent and insightful and amusing as anything I've read about him on the web or in print anywhere.

C: Well, thank you.

K: Well, you're welcome. Now don't go Kanye Krazy on me! Stay grounded.

C: Don't worry. That's what I'm trying to do.

K: The question remains, Coretta. Whaddya need me for?

C: I need help. I just can't do this on my own anymore. This whole thing has gotten way too big, and I don't see it getting any smaller. I'm still in high school. And I want to go to college. A really good college. Like Harvard or Stanford.

K: Forget college.

C: Excuse me?

K: Forget about college for now. Don't bother with the applications. Finish high school, yes. But at the rate you're going, you're not even going to need college. Ride this thing out, Coretta. See where it takes you. In one year's time you won't even need to fill out the applications. You can go to Harvard *and* Stanford. At the same time. Go all James Franco if you want.

C: Wow, Karl. You sound *not at all* like my parents. Or like someone who actually went to Harvard.

K: Well you can always defer for a year if you get in.

C: Thank you. Now to answer your question. How do I feel about hiring a middle-aged white man to help me write my black girl blog? I feel weird about it.

K: Me, too.

C: More than weird. I feel deeply unsettled.

K: Me, too. But the world isn't as black and white as it used to be, is it? Look around. It's pretty much full spectrum. Black and white still matters, of course— more than it ever should, though not as much as it used to. The best I can do is honor your voice. All that being said, I can totally understand if this is an issue for you. It would be strange if it wasn't.

C: It is an issue. Of course it's an issue. It's unethical, it's scandalous, and I'm more than slightly uncomfortable about the level of secrecy surrounding our arrangement. But secrecy aside, there's something about hiring you that feels safe in a way.

K: That's good. That's a relief, actually.

C: Because say I enlisted a young woman, especially a young black woman, to take on my voice, I would have to trust that she wouldn't take *over* my voice, usurp my followers, highjack my identity . . . or worse, expose me as a fraud. Oh my God! Listen to me. I sound like Lady Macbeth. See what I mean? I'm, like, losing my mind.

K: You are not losing your mind, Coretta. You are wise to be cautious and concerned. This is a big deal. So that brings me back to my first question. Let's talk about what you want me to do for you.

C: Well, for starters, thank you. It's just good to be able to talk about all this stuff with someone.

K: Someone besides Noprah?

C: Huh?

K: Never mind. We can discuss that later. You're welcome. Now let's put me to work on *Little White Lies*.

C: Okay. Yes. First of all, if you have some ideas for better organization or formatting, I'd love to hear those.

And I'm sure I could use some tips on Twitter. Tweeting is definitely not my forte.

K: Did you just use the word "forte"?

C: And I can use ideas for my big posts, although I guess that hasn't really been a problem so far. And well, you're a ghostwriter, right? That's what you do. You write for other people. So I guess I'd like you to do that. I mean, I would have to approve whatever you wrote before it went up on the blog.

K: Exactly.

C: And I would want to approve whatever you planned on writing before you wrote it.

K: Okay.

C: And of course I'll have the option to edit or alter anything you write before posting it.

K: Of course. Coretta, *Little White Lies* will always belong to you. It's your creation, and you should have the final word on whatever goes in it. My sole purpose is to support you. Whatever I write for you will be written for *you*. And it'll be your prerogative to alter, edit, change, delete, or obliterate anything I submit.

C: Oh. Okay. Cool. Oh, hey, can I call you back in a second?

K: Ha, okay. That was abrupt.

C: My mom wants something. I'm a kid, as much as I try to forget. She needs me to take out the garbage. Okay, I'll call you right back.

CHAPTER SIX

Coretta (December 3, 2013)

I was lying. My mom didn't need me to take out the garbage; she wasn't even home. I just got overwhelmed on the phone with Karl. I was talking to a real-life adult man about helping me with my blog.

Did I say white man? We wanna say it doesn't matter, but like he said, we know it does.

I was also overwhelmed because I didn't know whether to tell Karl about Pulse TV. I felt like if he knew about all that, it would make me more vulnerable to him. I'm not sure how, but it just would. He was a grown-up. He knew things that I didn't. He seemed like a nice guy, but he was a ghostwriter, and that seemed weird in general, right?

Okay, it was decided: I wouldn't tell him about Pulse TV. I mean, if I wasn't telling Rachel Bernstein—the girl who'd hooked me up with Karl in the first place via her mysterious connection with AllYou™, the girl with whom I became blood sisters at age eleven (while using a dull-as-hell pocket knife to cut our palms)—I surely wasn't telling Karl Whoever.

I took a few deep breaths, got a coconut water from the fridge, and returned to my room to call him back.

• • •

Note from Coretta: To Karl's credit, I, too, will use his abbreviations for the sake of expediency.

K: Yellow.

C: Okay, sorry 'bout that.

K: No problem. Now what else?

C: Well, if you could help me with the "Dear Coretta" letters . . . I mean, I wish I could answer all of them, but there's so many coming in that I barely have time to read them.

K: I could give that a shot. Let's hear one.

C: Right now? On the phone?

K: Yeah. Right now. On the phone.

C: I thought you hated the phone.

K: I do. But this isn't so bad. And it's relevant to how I work.

C: Okay. Here's one that just came in today.

Dear Coretta,

I'm a white boy, aged sixteen, and I live in New Jersey. I recently changed schools from a mostly-white school to one that's more mixed. For some reason most of my friends at my new school happen to be black. I honestly don't know why. It just kind of happened. I don't try to act black. I like rap music and stuff, but everyone does. Well, some of my new friends have started saying I'm a quote-unquote "honorary N-i-asterisk-asterisk-a." Sometimes they even call me that, as in, quote, "What up, N-i-asterisk-asterisk-a?" end quote, or quote, "What up, N-word!" end quote.

My question: does my new honorary N-word status give me the right to start using that word when I'm hanging out with my black friends?

Yours truly,
Honored

K: Really? That's a real letter you got from a reader?

C: Yes, an email.

K: Is he saying that his black friends are calling him "nigga," or are they calling him "N-word"?

C: Um, I think, both?

K: Like, the actual N-word, or are they literally calling out, "Hey, N-word!"?

C: I'm not sure?

K: Okay, here we go.

Dear Honored,

In a word: no.

Now that's an n-word we can all feel comfortable using. And "N-word"—as stupid as that sounds—is exactly how you should refer to the word in question, even when using quotation marks. No asterisks, no alternative spellings.

I am sorry, esteemed white people (honorary N-words included), but you are not allowed to use the N-word under any circumstances. It's really not up for discussion.

Furthermore, you have no jurisdiction over usage of the N-word by We the Black People, so please refrain from any discussions regarding when it is and is not appropriate for the N-word to be used by us.

With compassion,

Coretta White

P.S. Please remove the word "wigger" from your colloquial vocabulary as well. Thank you.

C: Hey, that's not bad. I like the "We the Black People" part.

K: It's yours. If you forward me the kid's letter, I can type it in for you. What else you got?

C. Wow. You are good.

K: Thanks. It's fun. How many of these letters do you get a day, anyway?

C: Usually between seventy-five and a hundred. That's

after they go through this automated trash and authentication filter.

K: Every day? And you read them all?

C: I try to, yes.

K: Well, that has to stop.

C: What?

K: Coretta, you can't be required to read about the individual problems of a hundred troubled teens every single day. Not to mention feeling compelled to give them advice.

C: I know. It *has* gotten out of hand. I don't know what I was thinking when I started answering them. I guess I just wanted to help. You wanna try another?

K: Really? Sure.

Dear Coretta,

I'm a freshman girl, and I just got asked out by a really hot senior guy. When I told my mom about the date, she said I wasn't allowed to go out with a senior. I told her she was being a hypocrite, since she is ten years younger than my dad, and that I'm old enough to make my own decisions, so I'm going out with him anyway. Am I right?
—Fourteen and Fierce

K: Fourteen and Fierce, huh?

C: That's her name.

K: Okay.

Dear F&F,

No, you are not right. You're fourteen years old. You should be old enough to make many of your own decisions, maybe even most of them. But not all of them—especially as long as you're living under your parents' roof. I'm not able to make all of my own decisions without consulting my parents first, and I've got three years on you. And I'm the one you're writing for advice.

First of all, the older you get, the more entitled you are to being a hypocrite. And having kids basically grants you a lifetime license to practice hypocrisy. So forget about playing the hypocrite card.

Now if you really thought you were entitled to date any guy you please no matter his age, then you probably wouldn't have told your mom about the date in the first place. Unless you thought she would approve, given your parents' vast age difference? Hmmmm . . .

Time is relative, F&F. My father is ten years older than my mother, too, but they met when he was thirty-eight and she was twenty-eight—she was twice your age and had ten-plus years of dating experience. Senior guys who date freshman girls are at worst predators and at best losers. And it's not always easy for a freshman girl to recognize that.

So, F&F, if I were you, I would try to think of your mom's rule as good advice and stick to dating guys your own age, at least until your second year of college. Then anything goes, right, Mom?
With love,
Coretta

C: Hey, that wasn't bad. Very earnest. And you even knew my parents' exact age difference . . .

K: I'm just riffing. But yes, I'm diligent. And that's how I write—fast. I can tell that's how you write, too. Which is good. And like I said, everything I write will go through you first before it gets posted.

C: Okay. So how will that work?

K: I'll send everything to you, you make whatever changes you want, and you post it yourself.

C: Sounds simple enough.

K: And if for any reason you want me to post something, I'll send it to you for approval first. You can tell me whatever changes you want, and then I'll put it up.

C: Great.

K: Anything else?

C: I barely have time to read other people's tweets, let alone retweet them.

K: Perfect. I can keep my eye on Twitter for you, and when I see something you should like or retweet, I'll send you the link. I'd also like to see you more involved with Black Twitter.

C: Black Twitter?

K: You don't know Black Twitter?

C: Is that a hashtag or a community?

K: Oh, it's both. And girl, you need to get yourself to Black Twitter *right now*!

C: I'll definitely check it out. By the way, you kinda sounded a little bit black just then. Oh, and slightly gay.

K: So you're a racist and a homophobe.

C: Impossible. My best friend is white.

K: All right, then. It was nice talking with you. Call me anytime, day or night. But I much prefer text or email.

C: Got it! Anything else?

K: One more thing: the level of secrecy you mentioned? It's absolutely essential for our arrangement to succeed. Now I'm sure that AllYou™ had you sign a nondisclosure agreement. That shit is for real. You cannot tell anyone that I or anyone else is helping you with *Little White Lies*. ANYONE. Understand?

C: Yes, sir!

K: I'm sorry to get all heavy at the end here. If you do ever feel the need to reveal anything about our arrangement, just make sure you consult with AllYou™ before you do. Same if you want to terminate our arrangement. As long as you're professional about it, I'm not going to take it personally. The most important thing is for you to stay true to yourself. I'm here to help, that's all.

C: Thank you.

K: Thank you, Coretta. See you in the cloud.

C: Bye, Karl.

CHAPTER SEVEN

Coretta and Karl (December 13–18, 2013)

Fri, Dec 13, 2013; 12:03 a.m.

K: you awake?

C: yes

K: why?

C: writing a paper

K: due tomorrow?

C: of course. Just started it.

K: on what?

C: civil war in Syria. For my geopolitics seminar

K: check Instagram

C: for what?

K: Beyoncé

C: what?

K: just have a look, please. Over & out.

tumblr.
LITTLE WHITE LIES

December 13, 2013

Little White Lie of the Day: "Beyoncé is middle management at the Bank of Satan and recruiting teenagers for summer internships."—The Five Most Popular Beyoncé Conspiracy Theories (mashable.com)

THE BEYONCÉ CONSPIRACY has nothing to do with the Illuminati, a Dutch Giant, Jay Z, or baby Blue Ivy (although Jay and Blue are definitely involved).

While you were sleeping, Beyoncé—under the cover of darkness, like a beautiful brown bootylicious Banksy—unleashed her latest creation upon the world. No press, no promo, no leaks. Just 14 new songs and 17 new videos, all part of her new "visual album" simply titled *Beyoncé*.

While I do possess an open mind and a healthy dose of skepticism, I have not yet fallen prey to any of the leading conspiracy theories of our time. But if the most popular entertainer alive can make an entire album (including 17 videos!) without *anyone* spilling the beans, well then, for all I know, 9/11

may have been an inside job after all. I'm kidding about 9/11;
please don't write me about it.

Mom and Dad claim that my first words were "mama" and
"dada"—in that order—but that's not something I remember.
However, I do recall that the first pop song I ever sang along to
was "Say My Name" by Destiny's Child. The associated image
of my mother rolling her eyes and wearily shaking her head will
be forever etched in my memory. She didn't get Beyoncé then,
and she still doesn't get her now. Which may be one reason
I've stayed so loyal to Bey. Of course I love my mother dearly; I
respect her; hell, I even *like* her. But I was never the sort of kid
to suffer the humiliation of being chaperoned to see my favorite
singer in concert. Some things just aren't meant to be shared
with one's parents.

Mom, to her credit, parlayed Beyoncé into teachable
moments. I learned about the wonders of hair extensions at
a remarkably young age. My mother also enlisted Beyoncé to
educate me about the appropriate times to wear clothes and
when it was okay to just walk around in your underwear. And
before I even started school, Beyoncé helped me comprehend
the nuances of the word "naughty."

My mother never tried to steer me away from Bey, either. She
accepted the Beyoncé phenomenon the same way she did boy
bands, the color pink, and princesses—as an immutable force of
influence on her daughter from which there was no way to shield
or protect her, but which would surely diminish. (In recent years,
I've tried to keep my continued Beyoncé worship from her. I've
indulged alone or with my best friend, Rachel. I also recently
invented the statistic that Americans between the ages of 12 and
48 are exposed to images of Beyoncé an average of 3.4 times
per day.)

The first CD I ever owned was her solo debut *Dangerously*

in Love. Mom bought it for me. I remember, because it got released the day before my seventh birthday. Even though my official birthday was still a day away, she took me to Target after school—no doubt to shut me up about it.

At least I've outgrown princesses, boy bands, and the color pink.

But Bey is still my boo. I don't own any of her other CDs, but I've purchased all her other albums on iTunes, and with my own hard-earned money. I know she doesn't need my money. But she has given me and the rest of the world so much over the years—not just as an entertainer but as a paradigm of power, confidence, beauty, and strength for black women to emulate— that I believe paying for her music is the least I can do to show my respect and support. Perhaps I'm an unwitting victim of the Beyoncé conspiracy, after all.

So when I got the "SURPRISE" Instagram message just after midnight, I had no choice but to dive in headfirst. Geopolitics paper be damned. My amateur analysis of the Syrian civil war can wait. As of right now, this night belongs to Beyoncé. And because of my newly standardized Blog Before Homework policy (jk, teachers! ☺) I have no choice but to devote these remaining hours of darkness to exploring the 14 songs and 17 videos of Beyoncé's "secret" album. Of course I'll be sharing my thoughts about the songs and videos with you, dear reader, in my first all-Beyoncé installment of *LWL*.

Please bear with me, as I am very much a novice at writing about music. I may have written a few clever lines about Kanye, but I've never even attempted to write a proper music review. And that's not what I'm about to do here. Rather, I will share my immediate impressions of the work at hand. I may not even write in complete sentences. But hey, it's the Internet. And it's very late and getting later.

Btw, since *BEYONCÉ* is being touted as a "visual album," I'll focus on the videos and leave writing about the songs to the millions of music critics out here in the blogosphere. Now without further ado, let's do this!

Note from Karl: Dear reader, if you wish to see more of the Beyoncé post—and trust me, it's worth it—please consult Appendix 2 on page 251.

Friday, December 13, 2013 (Gchat):

Coretta White - 3:12 PM
hello there

Karl Ristoff - 3:12 PM
well hello
so what did you think?

Coretta White - 3:22 PM
I liked it.

Karl Ristoff - 3:24 PM
You did? whew. We are talking
about the Beyoncé conspiracy, right?

Coretta White - 3:24 PM
yes. ha

Karl Ristoff - 3:24 PM
Any feedback from your pals at school?

Coretta White - 3:25 PM
Did you write that with your opinions or what you
thought mine would be? Everyone at school freaked
out about it.they woke up to find that the album had
dropped, and also that LWL had covered it overnight

Karl Ristoff - 3:26 PM
That stuff about your mom was
completely imagined of course
but if it was way off, I figured you'd change it.
was surprised at your light editing touch

Coretta White - 3:26 PM
I actually did have beyonce albums when
I was young . . . but I never liked pink. My mom asked
me about that, and I said I just added it for layers
My favorite color was and is gray.
I imagine yours is green

Karl Ristoff - 3:27 PM
It is. Not that I'm obsessed with making
money, but I do enjoy spending it.
How'd your paper go?

Coretta White - 3:28 PM
meh, nothing to write home about I think my
teacher was impressed because of the blog
post so thanks for getting me points!

Karl Ristoff - 3:29 PM
I hear that. What did YOU think of the Beyonce album?
And all those videos!! you're welcome!

Coretta White - 3:29 PM
I think Beyonce is making a statement

Karl Ristoff - 3:29 PM
it was fun to write. not easy, though

Coretta White - 3:30 PM
and she is changing her image

Karl Ristoff - 3:30 PM
What is her statement?And from what to what?

Coretta White - 3:30 PM
it was that she was just the queen, and there was no
need to talk about others. Now i think there is an
underlying theme of "I'm the baddest bitch.
WHAT" And I'm a bad bitch, nasty bitch,
queen bitch, lady to J-Hova

Karl Ristoff - 3:31 PM
She is a bad bitch for certain.

Coretta White - 3:31 PM
and classy of course I think
she is now just a representation of
every side of a woman that is desirable

Karl Ristoff - 3:32 PM
Yeah, maybe there's some healthy rivalry
going on between them, too. that's going keep both of
them motivated as individuals, and even stronger
as a team. She def covers a lot of bases.

Coretta White - 3:32 PM
Never stops.I'm not like beyonce I'm like . . . Demi
Lovato or something just waiting for a breakdown

Karl Ristoff - 3:33 PM
Ha, Demi Lovato?? Her people wanted me to tweet for
her, but they wanted me to audition, and I wasn't into it.

Coretta White - 3:34 PM
good choice on your part

Karl Ristoff - 3:34 PM
See, I do have some standards.

Coretta White - 3:34 PM
"rehab is great! dolphins!"

Karl Ristoff - 3:34 PM
Tweet that! @demilovato

Coretta White - 3:35 PM
Are you going to tweet for me?

Karl Ristoff - 3:35 PM
I think you need to chime in on black twitter with
some of this beyonce stuff too. I just stayed up all night
writing that blog! You tweet. Bt is on fire today.

Coretta White - 3:35 PM
"black twitter" OK, I will tweet.i'll remind you
that I'm going through puberty and high
school right now it's on fire about bey?

Karl Ristoff - 3:36 PM
oh yeah.

Coretta White - 3:36 PM
i suppose i should fan the flames

Karl Ristoff - 3:37 PM
fan em for sure. And also, see what people are saying,
and especially what they're rt'ing. If you see stuff you
like, or someone whose voice resonates, rt rt rt!

Coretta White - 3:38 PM
Will do. I'm not very familiar with twitter (gah, I know)
Feel free to monitor my progress

Karl Ristoff - 3:38 PM
The key is to get in and get out quick. No point lingering,
it's a terrible time suck. You'll do great. You are great.
I should let you get back to school and adolescence.

Coretta White - 3:40 PM
They are both quite time-consuming drags I should
let you get back to . . . .? writing for people?

Karl Ristoff - 3:41 PM
let's leave it at "?" see you in the cloud

Coretta White - 3:42 PM
nebulousbye

Karl Ristoff - 3:42 PM
bye! :D

Saturday, December 14, 2013 (Gchat):
Karl Ristoff - 1:58 PM
Peter O'Toole died today.
Though I guess that has
nothing to do with LWL.

Coretta White - 1:57 PM
Yeah, I don't think it does. Are you a big fan of his?

Karl Ristoff - 1:58 PM
I'm a fan of his name more than his work
Anyway, never mind. Nice work on the bey tweets

Coretta White - 1:59 PM
I just pulled up his wikipedia I've maybe
seen Lawrence of Arabia. OHHH da tweets!

Karl Ristoff - 2:00 PM
yeah, 8 nominations for Best Actor. Never won!

Coretta White - 2:00 PM
Yeah, I was trying to be clever.

Karl Ristoff - 2:00 PM
you are clever. yet not shallow. back to biz.

Coretta White - 2:00 PM
You really can only like Beyonce on social media.
I love that hbo documentary. She works really hard.
When she was talking about her dad in the
back of the SUV. Oy.

Karl Ristoff - 2:04 PM
Oy? You never told me you were Jewish.
But Beyonce was also able to convince me that
she is an authentic human being. A real person.

Coretta White - 2:04 PM
Yes, and if she isn't, then she is even more impressive.
The album coming out of nowhere made a little more
sense. And my best friend is Jewish.

Karl Ristoff - 2:07 PM
Could you imagine having your dad be your manager?

Coretta White - 2:07 PM
NO. Well, yes, and no. sometimes i feel like he is my
managerI just have no money to manage

Karl Ristoff - 2:08 PM
Ha, right. Won't be long though . . .

Coretta White - 2:08 PM
She had to pretend not to be the very best in
destiny's child. be humble and pretend she didn't
know why she's the one getting the interviews.
It's like Justin Timberlake and N'Syncit's
awkward until they really are just a solo artist

Karl Ristoff - 2:09 PM
Right! They seem to eventually break out and do
their thing. And then the good ones
maintain without self-destructing.

Coretta White - 2:10 PM
ExactlyLet's neither of us self-destruct. So why are you
so into beyonce? You're a walking contradiction.
I assume you can walk, but i guess I don't know.

Karl Ristoff - 2:14 PM
Oh, I'm just in a 5-day Bey phase.
This too shall pass. I am fully ambulatory. I can walk
away from Beyonce at any moment

Coretta White - 2:16 PM
I just mean that you're a middle-aged
white guy who is really into beyonce

Karl Ristoff - 2:16 PM
I know what you meant. There are tons of middle-aged
white guys into beyonce. Most of them are gay.

Coretta White - 2:18 PM
I guess I need to expand my circles.
I can't wait for college.

Karl Ristoff - 2:18 PM
Yeah, you'll meet tons of middle-aged
gay dudes in college. They're called professors.
Kidding, of course! Though come to think of it,
most of my favorite professors were gay.

Coretta White - 2:20 PM
HAHAHAHAHAHAHAHAHAHAHAHAHAHAHA
I don't know why that's funny, but it is.
Let's hope I get into a college

Karl Ristoff - 2:20 PM
As I like to say, "Love making gay jokes.
Hate homophobia."

Coretta White - 2:21 PM
That's the next blog post . . . kidding of course.

Karl Ristoff - 2:22 PM
Why? Cuz that's not bad

Sunday, December 15, 2013 (Gchat):
Karl Ristoff - 2:22 pm
You going to watch the Mandela funeral today?

Coretta White - 2:23 PM
I'm not planning on watching it I will read coverage and
watch videos. I've studied apartheid it's ludicrous

Karl Ristoff - 2:24 PM
I think the perspective of someone who has grown up
post-apartheid might be pretty compelling

Coretta White - 2:24 PM
I want to see the movie. eerie timing, right?

Karl Ristoff - 2:25 PM
Yeah. Not sure if I'll go or not. I do like Idris Elba
though—come on, The Wire???

Coretta White - 2:25 PM
I've never seen the wire. My parents probably
wouldn't want me to watch it.

Karl Ristoff - 2:25 PM
Sometimes i forget I'm chatting with a 17-year-old

Coretta White - 2:26 PM
I never forget I'm chatting with a
40-something white man

Karl Ristoff - 2:27 PM
On Internet dating EVERYONE watches the wire. HA HA

Coretta White - 2:27 PM
YOU DATE ON THE INTERNET?

Karl Ristoff - 2:27 PM
I mean, HA HA what you said about not forgetting
who I am. How else am I gonna get a date?

Coretta White - 2:27 PM
Tinder, OkCupid, Match

Karl Ristoff - 2:28 PM
Wait, how do YOU know about these sites, young lady??

Coretta White - 2:28 PM
I don't know what you look like . . .
so I guess if walking around and asking
someone out isn't an option . . . or FB . . .

Karl Ristoff - 2:28 PM
I'm not sure I want to get involved with your FB page.
Certainly not your personal page—do you even do face-
book besides LWL? How could you have time?

Coretta White - 2:31 PM
I have a FB page i link my LWL posts to it
It also helps because my friends share the links,
which helps it spread. My parents look at
my FB page, so it's super boring

Karl Ristoff - 2:32 PM
let's not be friends ok?

Coretta White - 2:32 PM
ahahahah, yes, let's not be friends

Karl Ristoff - 2:32 PM
Right: let's not friend each
other in the FB sense.

Coretta White - 2:32 PM
I think the less ties we have, the better, right?
You're like a genie

Karl Ristoff - 2:32 PM
FB is going to be over soon anyway.
Yeah, let's keep it business.
Keep it direct message only.
I'm trying to slim down.

Coretta White - 2:33 PM
Are you fat?

Karl Ristoff - 2:33 PM
Oh you mean genie,
like, magical?

Coretta White - 2:33 PM
yes I just mean you appeared out of nowhere
and you are helping me like a magical genie
I don't see you as a fat genie though

Karl Ristoff - 2:34 PM
Oh, well. Happy to help.I'm not that fat.
Just kinda husky. Think about Mandela! Think about
gay stuff too!I mean, you know what I mean.

Coretta White - 2:38 PM
I will think about all gay stuff

Karl Ristoff - 2:39 PM
LBGT is the new vanguard of civil rights. just sayin . . .
I mean LGBTQ anyway, we can talk about gay stuff later.
keep on keepin' on . . .

Wednesday, December 18, 2013 (Gchat):
Karl Ristoff - 3:39 PM
Yo what's up with Target?
I just saw a thing on Pulse TV about them not
carrying the Beyonce album after her flash release?
Okay, I know, enough about Beyonce.

Coretta White - 3:40 PM
I don't watch Pulse TV.
I think I'm going to write something
on the Obama selfie/Mandela story

Karl Ristoff - 3:41 PM
Good idea! You really don't watch Pulse TV?

Coretta White - 3:41 PM
The selfie story seems really relevant.

Karl Ristoff - 3:41 PM
Totally relevant. This is the year of the selfie isn't it?
And that was like Selfie of the Year.

Coretta White - 3:42 PM
I haven't seen the actual selfie,
only a picture of said selfie
I hope it was good. If my mom caught me
taking a selfie at someone's funeral . . .
Oooo lawd

Karl Ristoff - 3:43 PM
Is it online? You've got to friend that white lady!
Yeah, selfies at funerals. Not a good look.
Even for Heads of State.
Or maybe, especially for Heads of State.

Coretta White - 3:45 PM
Yeah, but I'm also going to work on stuff on Mandela . . .
you know, since it's quite a bit more important

Karl Ristoff - 3:46 PM
Have you noticed they tend to crop
out the white guy in that photo of the
offending selfie? Maybe to make room
for Michelle's reaction . . . I wonder if he's
cropped out of the selfie itself.
You're right. In the grand scheme of things,
Mandela trumps Selfie.

Coretta White - 3:47 PM
it's all about the story to be told Michelle has to look
like a mean black bitch while barack schmoozes with a
blonde woman blonde: the whitest kind of woman

Karl Ristoff - 3:48 PM
Michelle does have a formidable resting bitch face.

Coretta White - 3:48 PM
i have resting bitch face it's a condition

Karl Ristoff - 3:49 PM
I have a pretty strong RBF myself. so is that the current
term for the expression we old people call ISS ("I smell
shit.")?

Coretta White - 3:49 PM
i think RBF is just people chillin out when I have resting
bitch face, im usually just thinking about what i want
for lunch and it results in my face looking rather unap-
proachablei don't have to see it so i don't care

Karl Ristoff - 3:51 PM
Ha ha. ANYWAY, I'll keep my eyes peeled for the
Mandela post. Please let me know if you want me to
take a look at anything . . .

Coretta White - 3:52 PM
if i write i'll just post it i think that will simplify things right?

Karl Ristoff - 3:52 PM
Yes. Just here to help. Not that you need it.

Coretta White - 3:53 PM
oh, don't be fooled, i do. winter break will allow me some
time though to catch up on things (i hope)i'm drinking coffee
now btw I think it tastes like garbage, but from the way adults
treasure it, I hope to one day not feel like I'm drinking soil

Karl Ristoff - 3:58 PM
Oh, don't drink coffee. It's a very expensive habit.

Coretta White - 3:58 PM
really? can't i have one vice?!!? i used to play
candy crush, but I can't do that while i'm busy.

Karl Ristoff - 3:59 PM
5 bucks for a latte? And one per day is never enough! You do
the math. Yeah, I'd advise you to stay off those game apps too!
But that's not my job. Wasn't I trying to sign off a minute ago?

Coretta White - 4:00 PM
oh, i'm not on a latte yet. I hope to stay on dunkin donuts
regular for a while! Yes, I think you were signing off.
let me know what you think of my post

Karl Ristoff - 4:01 PM
Will do. Stay clean and fly right!
I'll send you some ideas for things I might write . . .

Coretta White - 4:01 PM
ok, great. until then . . . i'll sit here with my RBF

Karl Ristoff - 4:02 PM
Over and out.

CHAPTER EIGHT

Coretta and Karl (December 18–24, 2013)

tumblr.
LITTLE WHITE LIES

December 18, 2013

Little White Lie of the Day: 1) Barack Obama used his phone to take a selfie with the Danish prime minister. 2) First Lady Michelle Obama sat there the entire time scowling. 3) This is the part of Nelson Mandela's funeral that deserves the most coverage.

Nelson Mandela, the beloved President of South Africa, has passed away. I'm sure that all of you are aware of his passing . . . but I don't necessarily think it's because of all of the press covering all that President Mandela did to change the fabric of race relations in South Africa; rather, I think it's because of all of the press being dedicated to the "Obama Selfie."

1) We all saw the pictures of, well, the picture. President Obama is sitting with (blonde) Danish prime minister, Helle Thorning-Schmidt, and some dude named David Cameron

taking a selfie . . . at a funeral. This is not Obama's phone, not
that it should matter, but it's not his phone. Apparently the Danish
prime minister wanted to take a selfie with the US president and
that other dude. Now a day after the initial picture, the actual
photographer who took the picture said that the atmosphere
at this point was of singing and cheering to celebrate the life of
President Mandela, and that should and does matter.

2) The First Lady can be seen in many of the photos to be
scowling with her arms crossed. I want us to factor in some
things: a) She has been at a service for 2 hours (that would go
on for another 2 more), and didn't realize her picture was being
taken. We all have the right not to smile at all hours of the day.
b) There are pictures within the same very quick montage of
pictures where Michelle can be seen smiling and talking to
Barack (can I call him that?), the blonde woman, and that dude
(WHO IS HE AGAIN?). c) Maybe she has resting bit@# face, like
me and 70% of my friends. Who cares? Get out of her life and
facial expressions. d) Even if she didn't like the picture being
taken, THAT IS NOT THE POINT OF THIS FUNERAL SERVICE,
PEOPLE.

3) Nelson Mandela was wrongfully imprisoned for 27 years . . .
yes, 20 years + 7 years. Upon his release in 1990, he could have
done a lot of things, but what did he do? He picked up where he
left off and made strides to change race relations in the highly
volatile South African political sphere. These are the actions that
got him imprisoned in the first place.

In 1994 Nelson Mandela was elected president of South Africa,
becoming the first black chief executive in the country's history.
He broke down barriers of race and was beloved by blacks

and whites in his country. To really fathom the magnitude of his impact, you're going to have to leave this *LWL* post and do research of your own. Do this. That is what his legacy deserves.

Friday, December 20, 2013 4:05 PM

Tweet (Karl)

Target announces massive credit card breach 2 days after refusing to carry Beyonce album. Coincidence?? #Don'tCrossTheQueen

Thurs, Dec 20, 2013 5:05 PM

Coretta: Nice tweet.

Karl: Thanks. Any reason we aren't Gchatting?

Coretta: Any reason you didn't run that tweet by me first?

Karl: OMG, sorry! I totally spaced! Hope it wasn't a problem.

Coretta: Not a problem, just not the protocol we agreed upon.

Karl: You are correct. My bad. Won't happen again.

Coretta: Thank you.

Karl: Is anything else bothering you?

Coretta: Nope.

Karl: Okay. you sure?

Coretta: Yep.

Karl: Okay. Now that we're texting, I wanted to ask you: was that Mandela post based on something your parents said at breakfast?

Coretta: Gotta go, Karl.

December 24, 2013 (Gchat):
Karl Ristoff - 12:41 PM
Ok, so I realize you're not interested in being a gay rights activist, but I had to bring this to your attention: Heroic gay WWII codebreaker Alan Turing* was just issued a royal pardon for his crime of being gay.

Coretta White - 12:42 PM
ummm are you suggesting that I have a LWL post about that? I'm not trying to act like the blog is all about teeny bopper issues or anything, but seriously, Karl. That sounds like a PBS documentary. It's not like Hollywood is making movies about Alan Turing.

Karl Ristoff - 12:43 PM
But 3 days ago Uganda made it illegal to be gay!
And now Britain is pardoning a guy they castrated
60 years ago because he was gay?!!!

Coretta White - 12:43 PM
I'm writing for teens

Karl Ristoff - 12:44 PM
ok ok, you're right.
There are just so many gay teens in
the news these days.
From Hollywood to Uganda.

Coretta White - 12:44 PM
i'm not saying that we aren't going to write
about LGBT issues etc but I really don't think
that's the jumping-off point

Karl Ristoff - 12:45 PM
You're totally right. I knew it was a long shot.
I'll just pitch this stuff to Ellen.

Coretta White - 12:45 PM
HAHAH

Karl Ristoff - 12:46 PM
Yes. That was a joke.

Coretta White - 12:46 PM
Or Charlie Rose

Karl Ristoff - 12:46 PM
I appreciate the HAHAH
Charlie Rose is GAY??

Coretta White - 12:46 PM
I don't think so, but he would run that story
maybe anderson cooper is a better fit

Karl Ristoff - 12:47 PM
Oh. Yeah. Okay. You're right though. Xmas?

Coretta White - 12:47 PM
xmas? a story on the holidays?

Karl Ristoff - 12:47 PM
You did that hilarious piece about Thanksukkah!

Coretta White - 12:51 PM
LWL needs to be things that teens want to know

Karl Ristoff - 12:53 PM
Am I the only middle-aged white dude
who reads LWL? Might want to start thinking
beyond your core audience a little . . .

Coretta White - 12:53 PM
Yes, but not to the point of
losing the core audience

Karl Ristoff - 12:53 PM
Remind me. What is LWL?

Coretta White - 12:53 PM
LITTLE WHITE LIES<KARL
omg that means oh my GAWD

Karl Ristoff - 12:54 PM
I know what the letters stand for.
But what does Little White Lies stand for?

Coretta White - 12:54 PM
well, initially it was about the things my parents would
say flippantly that I didn't think were true it was
just a quick title i thought of now, it is more about the
little white lies everyone believes? maybe?

Karl Ristoff - 12:57 PM
You need to figure it out.

Coretta White - 12:58 PM
I don't need you to help me figure out the title of my blog.

Karl Ristoff - 12:58 PM
Not the title I'm talking about. I'm here to help if you
want, but maybe we should take a few days off.
You know, enjoy the holidays. Xmas and Kwanzaa and
New Year's and um, Boxing Day?

Coretta White - 12:58 PM
yeah, i'll enjoy kwanzaa of course

Karl Ristoff - 12:58 PM
I'm talking about YOU. Figuring out who YOU are.

Coretta White - 12:59 PM
Okie Dokie

Karl Ristoff - 1:00 PM
Happy Holidays!

Coretta White - 1:00 PM
FELIZ NAVIDAD

CHAPTER NINE

Coretta (January 3, 2014)

I'm looking at myself in the mirror, and while I think I look like the same girl that started this school year, I feel different. Same hair, same eyes, same resting bitch face, but not the same, either. Today is not like any other day. Today is the day that I will be going to meet with the Skool twins at Pulse TV . . . gulp. It's always been my dream to be able to miss school for something cool, something more legitimate than my precious education.

And suddenly here I am.

My parents not only are allowing me to miss school today, they actually insisted upon it. So if today is so special and such a big step in my life, why do I still feel like barfing into the sink? Nerves? Elation? The sinking feeling that I'm taking a royal crap on my friendship with Rachel? Whatever; I have things to do, and I will right this with Rachel in time. Maybe she can become my cohost or something. On second thought, national television might not be the best platform for her. But hey, I hear Ellen is a neurotic perfectionist, too, so who knows?

You know that feeling you get when you lie to someone about something, like they're going to show up at any moment? Well, I keep thinking Karl and/or Rachel are about to knock on my front door. Then I'd have to explain where I was going, and I'd start some stupid lie, and my parents would just blurt out the truth, and I'd be relieved and simultaneously mortified. Anyhoo . . .

I decided that to look the part, I needed to dress the part. Seeing as I was seventeen, I knew it wasn't necessary to wear a suit to have the Skool twins take me seriously. But my usual uniform of skinny jeans, combat boots, and a slanky sweater just wasn't going to cut it. I also didn't want to look overeager, like this was a college admissions interview or something.

Initially I tried on the dress that I wore to my sophomore year homecoming dance. My father thought it projected a young woman of class and grace . . . aka it had a neckline that looked straight out of the Renaissance period. Much more appropriate for a TV development meeting than a dance. Turned out I was not the same *size* girl as sophomore year, because there was absolutely no way my boobs were fitting into that dress anymore. It felt like I was being strapped in to go to space.

Aha! The dress that I wore to my cousin Derek's graduation from Brown last spring. Perfect. It was green, which spoke to prosperity. (Which made it Karl's favorite color for the same reason. *Hmm.* But at least it wasn't money green.) It was tailored, so I'd look professional. It was above the knee, and at my age, all dresses should be above my knee. And most importantly, my chest didn't look like a saran-wrapped deli sandwich.

Once I picked the dress, I took longer than usual to get ready, mostly to avoid talking to my parents. They were almost too excited about all of this. Don't get me wrong; I was excited myself. But parents' excitement feels weird, like it's going to jinx good things.

After that very strange dinner at Mike's house, I'd come home and told my parents about *his* parents' surreal proposition. It all came out in one big jumble, pretty much in one continuous breath. Mostly I remembered their faces glazing over with joy. I also remembered thinking, *You do understand that this is only happening because thousands of strangers are laughing at you and your breakfast-time foolishness. Or did you conveniently forget that?*

Maybe they had, because they snapped right into take-charge mode. They called Esther and Douglas Cornelius to thank them, and the four decided on the phone right then and there to accompany me to meet Anders and Karin Skool at the Pulse TV headquarters. (Which was only appropriate, like my tailored dress.) Mike wasn't able to get the day off from school, which was a bummer, but what can ya do?

All right, I'd restyled my hair about five times. Time to go out to the breakfast table. They were already waiting. My mother gave me a quick once-over. She had that same glazed look of joy once again. She just couldn't help herself, of course.

"I seem to remember that dress," she said, beaming. "It was for a certain graduation of a family member at a certain prestigious institution. I think that's good luck, you know."

"I didn't know you were superstitious, Mom." I was being slightly passive-aggressive. I do that when I'm nervous. Not my best quality.

"Well, I'm usually not, and I know you don't need luck today. I think you look very put together. Fierce, if I say so."

Why did she have to say "fierce"? Why did it bother

me? I know she was just being sweet and supportive, and if that's my biggest complaint, I should probably just shut up. So I did.

My dad cleared his throat.

"Now, Coretta . . ." I could tell he was going into a speech here. "I want to let you know that we're very excited to be a part of this venture with you. You've really grown into the woman we dreamed you to be, and then some."

Oh God, he's calling me a "woman" now. And if he only knew how much I'd let Rachel down, or that Karl even existed, he proooobably wouldn't be saying this.

Well, he didn't know. Only I knew the whole truth, and that was fine. It was fine. It was fine.

The more I say this to myself, the truer it becomes, right?

My father made his special pancakes for breakfast. My mother fixed her "special" bacon. She has mastered the art of crisping bacon—just for me. It's the little things in life. My parents let me drink coffee that morning, too. Dress the part, drink the part. I was the young woman of their dreams.

We took the train from Brooklyn to Manhattan. As I sat there, smushed between them, I realized that I hadn't taken the train into Manhattan with my parents in a while. I went with Rachel all the time. Well, not in recent months, but we used to go shopping, or just pretend we were twenty-three. Mike and I would go every few weeks, sometimes just to get a cookie from Levain Bakery. Using the word *cookie* is an understatement. If you haven't had one, get your life right.

So while I was feeling more grown-up than ever, I was also transported back in time. The nostalgia made my throat tighten and my eyes sting. *Not good.* But the memories kept shoving their way in: going in to see the ballet or a musical, or to gawk at the Christmas windows as a little girl. My parents might have been thinking the same thing, because they kept giving each other little smiles, and then smiling at me.

I smiled back. At least I wasn't crying.

The Skools' office was located in the heart of Times Square, generally a place I liked to avoid. Flashing lights, TV screens, and glass-plated TV studios were everywhere. My father (and his iPhone) navigated us through the masses of people (tourists with iPhones). A huge purple LED sign illuminated the outside of their headquarters: PULSE TV.

We walked into the lobby of the building where Esther and Douglas Cornelius were waiting for us, and so was . . . *Mike?*

Yes, that was him, planted next to his parents smiling at me. For a crazy moment, I felt like I was walking down the aisle (minus the nightmare of being married at the end). He stood in a sleek gray suit with a plaid tie and brown wingtip shoes. Damn, the boy cleaned up well. Apparently he thought it was the day for surprises.

I was glad he was there, but I wasn't looking for curveballs. I mean, the floor was made of marble, and I was wearing heels for the third time in my life. Baby steps.

We all checked in with the security guard, showed our IDs, and waited to be beckoned. As I tuned out my parents' and the Corneliuses' small talk, I no longer wanted to barf. In fact, I was feeling like I was right where I was supposed to be. The last time I'd felt this way was in the fifth grade, when I was spelling the final word for the Kings County spelling bee. I knew I was lucky to get *hypothalamus*, and I knew I was going to crush it. I did. (I also flubbed *episiotomy* at the state spelling bee, because I asked for a definition. Bad idea.)

Before I could dwell any more on past failures, a very tiny

twenty-something man in a suit and bow tie approached. His hair was so blond it almost looked white.

"Coretta, everyone, my name is Ethan," he said in the softest of voices. "I'm the Skools' assistant. Anders and Karin are ready for you now." With that, we all shuffled across the marble floors and headed into the elevator. The thirty-seventh floor. My ears popped.

Here. We. Go.

The doors opened on a mini version of the Pulse TV sign from out front. Whoever was in charge of decorating the office must have had short-term memory loss and needed to be reminded at every turn that they were still, in fact, at Pulse TV. We took a left and walked into what felt like a different world. There were no walls, no cubicles, only freestanding desks that were shared by lots of people—and everyone was wearing hoodies, skinny jeans, and combat boots. (Damn it, I could have worn my usual school clothes!) They were all smiling. Not what I imagined an office would be like.

Ethan introduced us to some of the employees (all seemingly his age) as we passed what must have been the break area. They played ping-pong, drank lattes, perused the Internet, and prepared smoothies at the juice bar. It didn't seem real. It felt like a movie set. Especially since when Ethan announced us, none of the employees offered their names in return. Everyone knew who we were. No, everyone knew who *I* was.

I looked at Mike and mouthed the words *"Oh, my God."*

Ahead loomed two offices with glass walls. My heart began to thump. On the other side of one of the floor-to-ceiling windows sat the Skool twins.

Karin and Anders were even more beautiful in person than on TV. Seriously, hauntingly so. Karin had grown out her blonde hair almost to the middle of her back. Anders's own blond hair was still short, crisply parted, slicked back. They both wore dark suits, impeccably tailored to fit their long, lean figures. So this is what the Swedish Adam and Eve would look like. If they weren't related, that is.

The twins were talking and laughing about something, but the glass must have been soundproofed, because even standing at the door, we couldn't hear a thing. Ethan knocked, and they both rose in unison.

It sounds strange, but the way they moved almost looked like the start to an interpretive dance. And not some garbage dance, but the kind on *So You Think You Can Dance,* the kind of earnest performance that would make you stand up and applaud the television. Maybe even cry.

I looked at Ethan. I had a terrible thought. They were so tall (Karin five-eleven? Anders six-four?), and Ethan was so small (five-one?), but they all had bright blond hair and striking, angular faces. He looked like their child. Their cute baby-man child. *Don't start giggling. Don't make a fool of yourself.* I drew myself out of my ridiculous brain and found myself shaking their hands.

"Coretta, we are so pleased that you are able to meet with us today. Everyone in the office is so excited that you're here." Karin had such a low voice for a woman. It was wonderful, calming.

I looked back through the glass to see that, in fact, everyone was excited. Staring, waving, smiling, saying things that I couldn't hear.

Anders chimed in. "Yes, we have been watching you for quite some time, ever since you two volunteered for our SKOOLS 4 ALL initiative. Everyone, please move with us into our conference room." As we moved, we walked past a framed SKOOLS 4 ALL poster—life-size. It featured the twins posing with a special "S4A" laptop they'd created for cheap and global mass production.

As I followed them through another glass door and into a hallway, Mike at my side, I tried to relax. In spite of their freakishly perfect dystopian Viking looks, *these were nice people.* Seriously; they gave laptops to poor African children, which apparently was like the Holy Grail of philanthropy (just ask my parents). And I'd first crossed their radar because of *that.* Maybe it even gave me cred. Maybe they really might think there was more to me than just my blog.

We went through a glass door that was on the side of that office into an actual hallway enclosed in glass, walked through another glass door into another office (Anders's), and then through another glass hallway and into a conference room. This room had a long, white, oval table. A ginormous TV with a perimeter of slightly smaller TVs surrounding it. A mini kitchen. The windows were floor to ceiling and looked out over Times Square. *Breathe.*

We all sat at the table, baby Ethan last. Without missing a beat, Karin resumed the discussion. "Coretta, my brother Anders and I are very impressed with your prose. We see you becoming a voice of your generation."

I had to sneak a glance at my mother. She made an *ohhh* face. Her eyes were watering.

"We were particularly impressed with your Mandela piece," Karin added.

"Yes!" Anders exclaimed. "And your post on Beyoncé! That was the clincher! Extraordinary!"

Everyone started laughing. I'm not sure what was funny, but I started laughing, too. Anders looked me in the eye. "The insight that you had on that album and all of those

videos, and on the phenomenon that is Beyoncé is unprece-
dented, especially for a seventeen-year-old. Coretta, my dear,
we envision Pulse TV as a platform for you to speak to your
generation, your millennials."

Are the millennials mine? I wondered.

"We think you are the teen Oprah meets Dr. Phil meets
Nikki Finke—with sass, smarts, and heart."

I bit my lip. I half-expected everyone to burst out laughing
again, but Anders was straight-faced. Was that a preplanned
line? I wasn't particularly taken by that description, but from
the looks on everyone else's faces, I was the only dissenter.

Anders went on to explain that each episode of the TV version of *Little White Lies* would start with a Little White Lie,
just like the blog. "Now what will be different is that all of
the lies need to be approved by Pulse TV, and your parents if
they like." Everyone once again erupted into laughter immediately after Anders did. A mini laugh track, only I was the
only one not getting the cue. "We want to use these 'lies,' or
subject starters, as the jumping-off point to segue into social
commentary, and more specifically into the personal one-on-
one counseling that you do so well. Your response to the girl
who was bullied had Karin, Ethan, and me crying."

The three of them nodded in unison.

Karin grabbed my hand in both of hers. Mine was cold
and damp with sweat, in contrast to hers, which were warm,
smooth, and perfectly moisturized without feeling the least
bit clammy. She looked into my eyes. "Coretta, we don't
want the world to have to wait any longer to see you and hear
from you. We would like to announce *Little White Lies* as
soon as possible. This will generate even more buzz for your
blog, which will trigger even more buzz for the TV show. We
want to start shooting mid-February. How does that sound?"

I started to formulate a response. Before I could, my dearest mother chimed in. "Perfect, as Coretta will have already heard from colleges by then!"

I looked at her to signal *back off, Mom*, but quickly took control of my face so as not to appear stressed. "It all sounds wonderful! Where do I sign?" I meant that as a joke, but Ethan started to shuffle out like a svelte Aryan hobbit. Apparently my absurd comments did not generate the laugh track.

Only then did it occur to me that Ethan was leaving the room *to grab an actual contract.*

My jaw must have dropped, because the twins stressed that I had nothing to worry about. I was about to become rich and famous whether I liked it or not. They said I just needed to keep doing what I've been doing. The only difference was that once I signed "the agreement," I (and now secretly Karl) would have to run every single post by them for approval. And those posts—while true to my voice (err . . . and Karl's?)—would need to focus on messages that would elevate teenagers in today's world: anti-bullying, acceptance of diversity, voter registration, and blah, blah, blah . . .

As I felt my eyes starting to cross and fought resting bitch face with all my might, my mother addressed the Skools. "Karin, Anders, thank you so much for having us all here today. I have to say, you have come to the right young woman to help elevate teenagers. Coretta, as I'm sure you found when she volunteered with SKOOLS 4 ALL, is an exceptional young woman with a unique vision for this world."

And just where did *that* come from? Had she rehearsed her lines, too? Whatever—it all sounded simple enough, provided nobody found out about Karl. All good things come at a cost, right? Isn't that what *The Lord of the Rings* is about?

Wait, how does that end? I didn't see them all. Who cares?

I needed this. Colleges would see this and want me, 3.7 GPA notwithstanding (it might have slipped to 3.5, but I can't bear to look).

Ethan shimmied back in and placed two contracts in front of me. They were several pages thick, written in tiny font. Ethan quickly flipped to the last page, nearly blank except for four signature lines: one for me, one for my legal guardian, one for each Skool. The twins each slid a pen across the table.

Karin said, "One contract is for you to keep; the other is for us. Both pens are yours."

I picked up one of the pens and signed.

After that I got lost in a cacophony of congratulations. Mike kissed my cheek and thanked his parents for orchestrating the deal. They kicked into Pulse TV–board-member mode and started to talk up my parents to the Skool twins. My parents were playing shy. My dad had his arm around my shoulder while he talked about me but not to me.

I was right where I was supposed to be, wasn't I? I deserved to be here. Sure, I didn't write the Beyoncé post, but I could have. And I wasn't in this room for that post, anyway. I was in here for the blog I created. Yes, I was receiving much-needed help. But even Oprah had help, tons of it.

Okay, if I was being honest, there was a teensy part of me that thought about the other place that I should be, could be. Rachel was single-handedly hosting the student council regional meeting. Everyone knew why I wasn't there, and nobody (but Rachel) was (or at least pretended to be) anything but happy for me. I'd texted her good luck before I left this morning.

Radio silence. Not even a response to wish *me* luck.

Now I had to go on a tour of the studio and meet the staff.

We had to start clipping along. It was fine. It was *FINE*. I knew she could handle it, so I probably didn't need to feel bad.

But, damn . . . I sure did.

Part Two: Winter 2014

CHAPTER TEN

Karl (January 6, 2014)

I woke up to a text from Alex. She told me to check my email. I hate it when people text me telling me to check my email. Who does this? (That's a rhetorical question. *Alex Melrose* does this.) If it's so urgent, just skip the email and send me a text in the first place!

And by the way, I get emails on my phone. So there's really no need to *text* me telling me about an *email*.

Anyway, was I cranky? Yes, I was cranky.

The email contained a link and nothing else. No "hi," no "hello," no "best," no "bye." No "Karl," no "Alex," no "K," no "A."

Really? This link is so urgent that you don't even have the time to preface it with a simple pleasantry? Not a second to spare for some semblance of an introduction, or a hint as to why this vital URL may be relevant? No? Just send me the link. Yeah, that's all you need to do. Because if it's coming from you, then it must be important. So of course I'll click on it IMMEDIATELY, no questions asked. I suppose you're right, Alex. Let's not waste our time with pleasantries.

It was an item on Deadline Hollywood, a site I visit every morning to take note of the latest undeserving prick to strike it rich with a rom-com screenplay about the loss of intimacy in the digital age. So I would have stumbled upon the piece within fifteen minutes, anyway. But hey, it was nice to be tipped off by someone I know and adore. And owe and abhor.

Teen Phenom Inks Deal with Pulse TV for *Little White Lies*

By **THE DEADLINE TEAM** | Monday, January 6, 2014 @ 7:30 a.m. EDT

Tags: Pulse TV, Coretta White, *Little White Lies*, Skool Twins

Coretta White, the 17-year-old web star behind the breakout teen blog *Little White Lies*, inspired by her Brooklyn power-couple parents Martin and Felicia White, has just signed an undisclosed deal with upstart cable/web network Pulse TV to create and develop a weekly television show based on the blog.

A press release from Pulse TV's co-CEOs Anders and Karin Skool, the 28-year-old billionaire twins renowned as much for their philanthropic efforts as for their aggressive business tactics, stated, "We are thrilled to welcome Coretta White into our growing family of young thinkers and doers, and we look forward to bringing *Little White Lies* to life for an even broader audience."

Good for her! So Coretta finally signed her deal with Pulse TV. Even though she claimed she didn't even watch Pulse TV. Had she been lying to me about that? Did it matter? Did any of this matter? Maybe not, but this *was* the moment we had all been waiting for. Given that the deal was being reported first thing Monday morning, the contracts had obviously been signed the previous Friday at the latest.

Well. It would have been nice if Coretta had wanted to share the news with me directly. It would have been nice if she'd even mentioned that this was a possibility way back when. Maybe when Alex had first discussed it with her? Maybe even Friday, as soon as she'd signed her first TV deal for the blog *that I was writing*? Or maybe as soon as she got home and popped the champagne—err, sparkling cider? Or at some point over the weekend?

No? No time to call Karl and tell him the good news?

Alex sent a second text. This one asked me to call Coretta ASAP to let her know that I knew the news. And to congratulate her.

Okie dokie.

True, I was The Help. I'd gone in knowing as much. How convenient, too; now I had the answer to the self-pitying identity crisis I'd suffered when I took this job. Who was Karl Ristoff? What was Karl Ristoff? Easy. *The Help*. This was my professional (and let's face it) personal identity. And as of late, I had to admit I hadn't been much help at all.

I'm not sure why I'd thought I could offer something more. It's not like Coretta and I were going to be pals. Or friends. We'd decided as much. Had I thought I could be some kind of mentor to this girl? Why would she want to follow the advice of a forty-one-year-old ghostwriter who sat on a silver yoga ball and trawled the web all day looking for memes?

If Coretta didn't want to explore serious issues beyond her own comfort zone, that was her prerogative. If she didn't want to grow and expand her audience, I'm sure she had her reasons. And they were probably good ones. The kid seemed smarter than me for sure—a lot smarter than I was at her age. If she wanted grown-ups telling her what to do, she could do a lot better than the Dark Lord of the Twittersphere. Her parents, for instance. Her dad was like Matthew Knowles, if he traded his God complex for a Harvard Law degree and a conscience, and her mother was Brooklyn's answer to Michelle Obama.

So it was just another job. And if I wanted to keep it, I had better schmooze my client.

I knew what I had to do (well, what Alex had commanded me to do), and I wasn't happy about it. It had been more than two years since I had actually initiated a phone call that wasn't for tech support or pizza. The last time was after I mistakenly tweeted as Alec Baldwin a photo of his then-fiancée, doing yoga. It was a big misunderstanding, and we later sorted it all out. (Though, come to think of it, I haven't worked for a Baldwin since.) But that call had to be made, per Alex's command, and so did this one.

Since it was her first day back at school after the winter break, I waited until the afternoon.

At 3:04 P.M., I picked up R$$P. Coretta answered right away.

C: Karl?

K: Congratulations!

C: Oh. Um. Thanks.

K: Oh, come on. Don't be so nonchalant. Your first TV contract! This is a big deal! I hope you've been celebrating.

C: A little. I drank a glass of champagne with Mike and our parents after we finished up at Pulse on Friday. And Mike took me to an amazing dinner at Per Se on Saturday. So yeah, I guess I've celebrated some.

K: Champagne and dinner at Per Se. I'd say that qualifies. Don't get me wrong; I would have been celebrating, too, if anyone had bothered to tell me about it. I had to read the deal report in Deadline Hollywood this morning.

C: Oh, Karl! I'm sorry. I totally should have shared the news with you. But I was so caught up in the weirdness of everything—the bigness, the strangeness of it all— the way everyone was treating me at Pulse. Like I was a cross between their newfound savior and their latest acquisition. Like I was their fancy new toy, and they couldn't wait to get me out of the package and start playing with me.

K: Wow. Pretty awesome.

C: Well, it would be a lot more awesome if I could get in touch with Rachel. I've been so rotten to her lately, and now she's not returning my calls or texts OR my emails, and she wasn't even at school today—

K: Coretta, I'm really not the person to talk to about Rachel. But like I said, congratulations. I mean that. And don't worry about not telling me sooner. I mean, at all.

C: Are you okay? You sound mad or something.

K: Not mad in the least.

C: Really? Because I'm sorry, what more can I say?

Between the insanity of Friday, and spending all weekend being worried sick about my best friend, I've been a little distracted, okay?

K: No, really. It's fine. This isn't about me. It's about YOU.

C: Thank you. And I'm glad you said that. I still need your help, Karl.

K: You sure about that?

C: What do you mean? Of course I still want you to help me. Everyone at Pulse loved your Beyoncé post.

K: Oh? Well, that's nice.

C: I'm serious, Karl. I still need you. But things are on a whole new level now. From today forward, I can't have you posting anything without getting my approval first. Understand?

K: We already had this conversation, didn't we?

C: Well, yeah . . . but things are different now. Everything that goes on the blog or on Twitter has to go through the proper channels at Pulse TV first.

K: Of course. It's Pulse TV. This is the big time.

C: Right. Well. Good. I'm glad you understand.

K: I understand perfectly.

C: From now on, every new blog will take the format of the TV show until we launch the actual show in March. After that, the show and the blog will be fully integrated. We will start with an issue that I select—with the help of the Pulse people, naturally.

K: Naturally.

C: Then we'll come up with a new Lie to fit the issue. I do my social commentary, inspired by the Lie of the Week. And finally, we bring on a kid who has a problem that's related to the issue. And I give them sort of one-on-one counseling.

K: Which you're qualified to do, based on the advice columns you've written for your blog.

C: Exactly.

K: Well. That sounds perfectly . . . perfect.

C: Yeah. I think it's going to be great. The people at Pulse were really into the stuff I did on bullying back in October. They've got a big anti-bullying initiative. So they're anxious for LWL to do a lot more with that subject.

K: It sounds like you're on the right track.

C: Thanks, Karl. I'm glad you think so. I'm really happy that you want to be on board for this. This is going to be so amazing! My own TV show.

K: Yep, your own TV show. Amazing.

C: I know, right?

K: Right. Anyway, I just wanted to wish you well and make sure everything is copacetic. Please let me know what I can do to help.

C: Thank you, Karl. I will. Let's talk soon, okay?

K: Yes, soon!

C: Okay, bye!

K: Bye!

Ahem. Not exactly a successful schmooze session. Coretta had failed to pick up on my very obvious sarcasm, but that wasn't the most annoying part. She sounded dangerously out of touch with who she was. Like she was trying to convince herself that she had done the right thing.

Maybe she really believed that. The old Coretta wouldn't have, but what did I know about the old Coretta, really?

It seemed to me that the best days of *Little White Lies* were already behind us. Still, I was contractually obliged to assist her via my conduit at AllYou™, one Alex Melrose. I was a professional. I was THE HELP. If Coretta White was happy to have her web platform hijacked by a creepy set of twins holding a giant sack of money, I was still going to be there for her. And if she and Pulse TV wanted more ammunition to wage their War on Bullying, then that was exactly what I'd give them.

Exactly.

CHAPTER ELEVEN

Coretta (January 8–10, 2014)

I woke up from a bad dream. I couldn't quite remember what it was or why it was bad. It was about . . . someone or something was coming to get me. I only remembered that I was running for what seemed like forever and didn't think I could run anymore. I woke up just when I was about to find out.

I had been having more nightmares as of late, but I guess that's what happens when you're hustlin' each and e'ery day.

That's a joke. Ha. Ha.

I was glad to be awake. I was glad to listen to the comforting, mundane, albeit odd sounds of my parents discussing whether they should finally redo the bathroom in the hall. Why is this a conversation one needs to have at 7 A.M.? We can't know.

I grabbed my phone to see what the world of social media had for me that morning. Another shooting in the news, Miley Cyrus did something else inappropriate, and then . . .

I saw, and barf rose up my throat.

tumblr.
LITTLE WHITE LIES

January 7, 2014

The Beauty of Cyber-Bullying

"Progress is impossible without change, and those who cannot change their minds cannot change anything."

—George Bernard Shaw

Today, instead of a Little White Lie, I'm going to start with the Truth.

A few months ago, I wrote my first-ever response to a reader seeking advice. The subject was bullying, and naturally my response came from an anti-bullying stance. Naturally. But I was so young then. Now that I am older, I am compelled to report that on the matter of bullying, I have decided to switch positions from *Con* to *Pro*.

Just for the record, I remain adamantly pro-choice (but still a virgin, Mom and Dad! Don't worry!), I still support legalization of marijuana (even though I've never tried it), and I continue to oppose the death penalty (haven't committed any violent crimes yet; fingers crossed!).

Some of you may be thinking, "*Pro-Bullying?!* WTF?" Please hear me out. And don't worry, I'm not going to waste our time together arguing all the most salient points my pro-bullying sistren and brethren have already well established, e.g.:

- Bullying serves an essential social function. It toughens kids up for the hard knocks they'll suffer for the rest of their grueling lives.

- Trying to rid the world of bullies is just another lame attempt at inclusion and equality along the lines of "everybody wins a trophy."
- Labeling bullies as "bullies" and victims of bullying as "victims" does more long-term psychological damage than the bullying itself.
- The best way to deal with a bully is to punch him in the nose; i.e., Stop Snitching and Join the Fight.

Now that we've made it through Pro-Bullying 101 (any converts yet?), I will proceed to the more subtle points of my reversal. Mine is *not* an ANTI-Anti-Bullying stance, but *PRO-BULLYING*. Specifically, I would like to concentrate on promoting dynamic new bullying possibilities thanks to a platform that I know a little something about: the Internet.

Let's no longer think in terms of Bullies and Victims; on the Internet, we are all potential bullies and victims. If you only take one thing away from this post, it's this: if we all work together, We Can Change the World with CYBER-BULLYING.

For starters, let's get rid of the noun and stick with the verb. (Technically a gerund, but gerund is not a word you want to throw around in conversation.) Let's stick with the all-purpose description of an action. Like "friending." If "bully" can become a word like "friend," CYBER-BULLYING can be the great new equalizer. CYBER-BULLYING takes the word away from the strong and puts it at the fingertips of the weak, the average, the powerless.

Like "friending," bullying used to require some form of real or perceived power. The classic playground bully uses his size and strength to intimidate and abuse. But plenty of other bullies wield more insidious sources of power: social status, socioeconomic advantage, sex appeal . . . much like "friends."

See what we did there? No more "labels."

Sure, CYBER-BULLYING may come easier and be more damaging if the aggressor has a large Twitter following. (Welcome to my Bully Pulpit!) But any one of my schoolmates can wreak plenty of emotional havoc with just 15 minutes and an anonymous email address. And just as power is no longer a prerequisite, weakness is no longer required of the bully's intended Victim. Or Target, if you will. With CYBER-BULLYING, you can target the strong as well as the weak. In fact, TARGET™ just got cyber-bullied a few weeks ago!

Don't like a corporation? Get online!

Don't like an entertainer? Get online!

Don't like a blogger like me? Get online!

Get online and start *BULLYING*.

If EVERYONE would just begin Cyber-Bullying IMMEDIATELY, with RECKLESS ABANDON, then before we know it, our entire online presence—both individual and collective—will be awash in a sea of senseless negativity. Dare I say we have already become awash in a sea of senseless positivity with "friending" and "liking"? Oh, yes; I have already said it.

As for those few voices—the lonely and truly sadistic cyber-bullies (lower-case), lurking in the shadows of their dark little rooms, eager to sling their sticks and stones—we will no longer give a damn about them. Only when WE ARE ALL CYBER-BULLIES will the slut-shaming blubberheads and self-righteous comments section hate patrol cease to exist.

A final thought: I was pleased to see a recent item on Pulse TV about their nonprofit NGO SKOOLS 4 ALL. Or #S4A, as you might know them on the Twitternets. They are launching an initiative to provide children in Africa between the ages of 12 and 18 with their own laptop computers. They are currently distributing brightly colored "portable schoolhouses" (a

euphemism for backpacks) through an ambitious "nationwide
pilot program" in the Central African Republic.

According to the #S4A website, each backpack will include a
rugged solar-powered laptop outfitted with a direct satellite Wi-Fi
connection, promising that "Soon, every student in every village
in Africa will be truly connected."

And seriously, folks, just imagine if every one of those
millions of lucky African children could use that shiny new laptop
for CYBER-BULLYING. We would all be that much closer to
becoming a World United as One.

While it is imperative to Think Globally, we also must Act
Locally. Which is why I urge each and every one of my readers—
yes, I'm talking to YOU!—to please START CYBER-BULLYING
TODAY!

What in the hell did "I" just write? Had Karl lost his mind?
I'd *just* told him that he couldn't write something without
my approval, which would then require the Skool twins'
approval. And of all things, he writes something in favor of
bullying? And promotes their nonprofit as a mechanism for
the spread of bullying?!

The ramifications of this post were beyond my capacity to
imagine. The Skools . . . well, I couldn't even go there right
now. I thought of the kids who read my Tumblr. They looked
up to me. They would be hurt by this. The teachers and administrators who endorsed me would feel betrayed. The parents,
oh God, the parents! Why didn't Karl think of the parents?!

My hands were shaking as I read it. My eyes felt like they
were coming out of my head. I *wished* my eyes were coming
out of my head, because that might mean that I wasn't actually awake to be experiencing the hell that was this blog post.
I dialed his number, and took a deep breath.

K: Hey there. I thought you might be calling . . .

C: What in the hell do you think you are doing? You wrote a pro-bully post? *Pro*-bully? Who does that?! And then you call out SKOOLS 4 ALL, which is something that actually does *good* in the world—

K: Coretta, calm down. I thought it was funny. I was using satire.

C: It wasn't approved, Karl! Take it down right now. Right now! No, I'll take it down. *You* don't do anything!

K: Coretta—

C: The Skool twins are going to kill me! And— OH MY GOD! I can't even take the goddamn post down! The site has crashed because of all of the comments it's getting! You shut down Tumblr! You . . . you . . .

K: Wait, Coretta? Coretta, are you crying? Don't cry, okay? Don't cry—

C: Shut up. I'm not crying. I have a cold. But Karl, the Internet lives forever, something I think you're keenly aware of.

K: It's just a post.

C: Just a post? G-g-go to hell. This is my life.

K: Your life. Okay. Gotta go, Coretta—

C: Gotta go? We need to fix this, Karl. Karl? Karl?!

He hung up on me.
Karl hung up on me.
That just happened.
My cheeks were on fire. If I were lighter-skinned, I think you'd see that I was blushing. My throat had a grapefruit in it. My stomach left my body. What was I going to do? How was I going to fix this?

I stared at my computer and waited for the server to respond. As I watched the refresh wheel continually spin, I talked myself down. It was going to be all right. As soon as the server came up, I would simply take down the post, and it would be fine. Shit happens, right? Right. Maybe I could make up something. Like I was hacked. On the other hand, lying about being hacked didn't turn out so well for Anthony Weiner aka Carlos Danger. Like me, he was another disgraced person my parents had once admired.

My cell phone started ringing. It was one of the Skool twins. I don't know which one, because when they gave me their numbers, I put them in as "Skool 1" and "Skool 2." Truth be told, it didn't matter. Both were equally terrifying in this situation. I did not pick up.

My phone filled up with voicemails.

Listening to the messages was not an option. I could not face them. What would the Skools say? What did they know? Why were they still calling? *You left a voicemail; stop calling!*

I closed my eyes, my phone still buzzing, and pictured my life swirling down the toilet.

There was only one thing to do. I told my mom I was too sick to go to school, then went back to bed and slept for nine hours. I woke up in a fog. Then I remembered my horrible morning. I had to call Rachel. Even with all of the resentment festering between us, the state of our friendship didn't compare to the shit storm that I found myself in. I needed a safe place. I needed a safe person. I couldn't go to my parents about this, not yet. It was too embarrassing. I declined another incoming call and dialed my friend.

R: Umm . . . hello? (She sounded bored. She really did not want to be talking to me right now, if at all.)

C: Rachel (sniff, sniff) . . . It's Coretta.

R: I know. Don't worry, your number is still in my phone.

C: I, I'm sorry, and I will get into all of that, but I need your help . . . I mean, I need your help again, like, right now—

R: Whoa, slow down there, girl. You're hyperventilating.

C: Did you see the blog this morning? I have a TV show thing, and I know I should have told you, like, months ago . . . Anyway, these twins are calling me, and they are, like, Vikings, but from the future, and I don't know what to do. This guy, the guy your connection set me up with, he helps me write. Umm, he is mad at me, and he messed it all up, and I, I, like, can't think—

R: Shh. I'm coming over to your house. You don't sound like you should be riding public transit. Are your parents home?

C: Yes. It's a school night.

R: Okay, just let me come to the front door, and I'll tell them we're working on a project. Stay in your room. And blow your nose. I can hear the snot dripping.

C: Okay.

It felt so comforting just to hear her voice. Like when you're a little kid and you go to your first sleepover, and it's all fun and games until it's time to go to bed. At that point you realize that you want *your* bed, with your parents in the room down the hall—not sleeping on the floor next to all these other kids in someone else's house. When your parents finally pick you up, you feel shame in leaving the party. But you don't care. You're going home.

By the time Rachel showed up, I was laid out on the bed, rubbing my bleary eyes at the computer. The server hadn't come back up. The post was just sitting there, staring at me, mocking me.

She quietly closed the door. Then she sat on the edge of my mattress. Once she looked at my face, I think she deserted any plans to let me have it. I was already defeated. Knocking me down would feel like punching a kitten.

Funny, the last time Rachel and I had a heart-to-heart was the last time I broke down over this blog, and here we were again. I wasn't sure if Rachel knew anything about Karl. She'd only introduced me to AllYou™, after all. And the woman at AllYou™, Alex Melrose, made me sign several agreements promising never to reveal Karl's identity or the nature of our relationship. So I figured I had to start from the beginning, for Rachel's sake.

It all came out in a rush, just as it had before.

I told her that at first Karl was there just to *help*. As Rachel had promised. And he *had* been helpful. The original idea was that he would guide me, and maybe write a little post here and there. At least, that was *my* original idea. But then the tables turned a bit when my most popular post (Beyoncé) was his, which led to a shift in our dynamic. I thought Karl was jealous of the recognition that I was getting from his—well, to be fair, "our" work. Now he was out to get me, sabotage me, defame me. (I was going to say "crucify," but that felt a bit much.)

I told her that by the time I met with the Skool twins I was determined to take charge of the blog again. They instilled this sense of power in me, and that I really thought everything was going to be okay. But when Karl found out about the Pulse TV deal, he responded with the pro-bullying post. He responded by getting pissed. At *me*. I don't know what I was thinking. Maybe I was hoping he would be more . . . I wasn't sure. *Grown-up*. But what did I know about grown-ups? My parents were unfathomable sometimes, too . . .

That's where I ended.

I looked at Rachel. She didn't say anything. I wanted her to tell me what to do. I half-expected her to tell me to get on a plane and leave the country. Sadly, that wasn't feasible for several reasons: I had no passport, I had no money (yet), and they'd probably stop me at the gate for being a traitor.

All of a sudden, Rachel grabbed my hand. It felt good for the same reason it felt weird: we hadn't spoken, much less hugged, in weeks.

"You know what you have to do," she whispered.

"Could you be more specific?"

"You have to come clean. You have to tell people before they find out. Trust me on this."

She was right. I knew she was right.

Besides, I had no choice but to trust her. She was the only person who knew the whole truth.

It took the two of us about a half hour of feverish back and forth to make the final decision.

I would write a confession. I would then email it out to the people in my life that would be most hurt by my lies. It was a small but vital list.

Moments later, I was sitting at my computer. Rachel stood over my shoulder, helping me craft the letter sentence by sentence.

As painful as it was to put it all into words, it was cleansing. What's the word? Cathartic. That sounds very hippie-dippie, but it *was* cathartic and cleansing, so shut up about it. I was fragile. My blog should've been called *Big Fat Black Teenager Lies*. Not that I was fat, but the lies were fat. Not that it would matter if I was fat. Never mind.

I hit SEND. Rachel squeezed my shoulder. Then she left.

Then I waited.

To say that I had a sleepless night would be an understatement. I didn't even bother getting under the covers. I was too twitchy. I felt gross, but also like a gross *person*. My subconscious wouldn't let me forget it. I needed to start being more of a warrior in my life and confronting my wrongs.

At around midnight, I grabbed my phone, that vessel for all things good and bad, and I listened to the voicemail from "Skool 1"—left right after the blog post from hell.

"Coretta, hello! It is Anders and Karin Skool here. We just wanted to ring you this morning to tell you that we loved your blog post on bullying!"

I'm sorry, what? Are they insane? Am I insane?

"We thought it was so funny! And to take such a satirical position on a serious subject affecting today's youth? So clever! Cheers, darling!"

I wondered for a moment if I'd really gone off the deep end, if I was dreaming or hallucinating. I'd sent out a confession email so as to distance myself from an inflammatory and offensive pro-bullying post. And I'd just discovered that it was all for nothing? Maybe the universe was out to get me. I was whispered a string of words, some that I'd never said before, and most that I hope not to repeat.

I had another voicemail from "Skool 2."

This one had just come in. Tonight. After I'd sent the confessional email. So this was it. I knew I was fired. I knew I was going down in flames. Hearing it would bring me back to reality.

"Coretta, thank you for your honesty. Karin and I wanted you to know that your secret is safe with us. We would also like to offer our reassurance that for the sake of our respective reputations—yours and ours, Coretta—we were able to take appropriate measures to prevent your confessional email from reaching either your parents, or your dear friend Michael and his parents. Just go back to writing your own material. Needless to say, we insist upon that. So don't let it happen again. Cheers."

Okay, something was seriously wrong here. That was it? *"Don't let it happen again? Cheers?"* That was all they had to say about what I did? And how were they able to intercept my email before it reached my parents and the Corneliuses?

Their smug demeanor and apparent control over my email terrified me. My mind whirled into the wee hours of the morning.. Thinking about it all, I realized that maybe the Skool twins realized that my secret would make *them* look bad. After all, they did have quite a lot of benefit from *Little White Lies* taking off. I was still guilty and gross, yes. But at least I wasn't going to be fired. At least my parents weren't going to find out. And neither would Mike or his parents. Not sure how that worked exactly, but it was both a relief and a serious brain twister. I could stop having to worry about reading some disparaging press release. Unless Alex Melrose or Kranky Karl decided to go public, which seemed unlikely. As the heavy weight lifted from my shoulders, I might have even managed to doze off before the sun came up.

It was 7 A.M. on Wednesday. Once I felt capable of at least *considering* putting on pants and leaving my room, I texted Rachel and told her to tell Alex Melrose to fire Karl.

Weirdly, I felt a surge of confidence. Maybe it was because Rachel and I were friends again. But I also thought, *what better time to write my first post for the TV show?* A nice fluffy celeb piece that would get people off my last post and on to thinking about someone else's life that doesn't concern them.

Little White Lies
True or false? Now more than ever, in the age of Internet democratization, the creation of celebrity and its power rests with us, the people.

CHAPTER TWELVE

Karl (March 15, 2014)

Pulse TV must have purchased exclusive rights to the word *truth*.

Ironic, given how I'd started my last post for Coretta. But fitting, too.

In the weeks leading up to the PULSE TV LIVE premier of *Little White Lies LIVE*, I had been bombarded with banner ads and pop-ups on every webpage, promising me "God's Honest Truth" if I tuned in. (Okay, to be truthful, that was one of the few truth-related phrases that *wasn't* used in the campaign.) But they trotted out nearly every other truth-based cliché:

TRUTH be TOLD.
Saturday, March 15
Little White Lies LIVE

Can you handle the TRUTH?
Saturday, March 15
Little White Lies LIVE

It was a strictly word-based campaign. Black and white. Bold face. Sans serif. Helvetica, to be exact.

TRUTH & CONSEQUENCES.
Little White Lies LIVE
Saturday, March 15

Occasionally one word, usually *WHITE* or *LIES*, would be written in white letters against a black rectangle.

Some ads were written in textspeak and/or had most vowels removed from the copy. I imagine to make it more teen-friendly.

TRTH 2 PWR
03/15/2014
LWL LIVE

In case you're wondering how I was doing: shitty.

For the past several weeks I had ordered delivery for every meal, mostly pizza and Chinese. I had left my apartment only to procure essentials—ice, toilet paper, ice cream, beer, and cigarettes—at the bodega down the street. And even during those brief half-block forays, I was still inundated with Pulse TV's "TRUTH."

Passing buses exclaimed:

THAT'S THE TRUTH, ~~RUTH~~ CORETTA!

Even my corner bus stop assured unwitting passersby:

The TRUTH shall set you FREE!
LWL LIVE.
MARCH 15. 8 P.M.
PULSE TV.

It was now the Ides of March, and the TRUTH was about to be revealed. While I didn't understand the strategy behind excluding Coretta's image from the network's marketing push, I was thankful for it. Being haunted by the face of the teenager whose brain I'd tried to inhabit (but whom I'd never met) had led to a series of unsettling nightmares (you should thank me for sparing you the details).

I still had no idea what Coretta's show was going to be.

I still had no idea if I was going to watch.

Okay, that's not the truth. Of course I was going to watch.

Things were quiet at the communications table. The phones were not ringing. Twitter was up on one of the big monitors, but I was more attuned to the Three Loco* video playing on the other one. So strange—I had farmed out all my celebrity ghost-tweet accounts at the beginning of the year in order to focus my creative energies on *Little White Lies*.

Since Alex had called (going on two months ago) to tell me that Coretta was firing me, I didn't have much work to do. I could return to g-tweeting whenever I wanted. But I was in no hurry—though every day I silently gave props to my previous clients for having the decency to keep their mouths shut about me. Mostly I stewed in self-righteous rage.

What the hell was up with that ridiculous confessional email?! Naming names! Not even blind cc'ing! The people on that list were *not* the kind of people whose radar I want to be on! The Corneliuses? The Skool twins? These were the Powerful. They might actually own and operate their own radar systems, for all I know. I imagined they'd all commence prying into my life immediately.

Thankfully when you googled "Karl Ristoff," nothing much came up. But the tentacles cc'ed on that email stretched well beyond Google. Last I'd heard, Pulse TV was developing its own search engine.

I still couldn't believe that the little genius had shit-canned me. And for what? Writing her biggest post since the Beyoncé Conspiracy? Oh, right, ummm . . . No. It was for *not following protocol*. Not clearing the post with her first, so she could clear it with her new sugar twins and make sure it jibed with their New World Order agenda.

But there's no way Coretta would have approved that cyber-bullying post. That is, the new *corporate* Coretta (*Corporetta?*) never would have. The old Coretta would have gotten it. Shit, the old Coretta would have written it herself. I started laughing out loud alone. (Never a good sign.) Here I was again, imagining that I actually *knew* something about this girl because of a Tumblr I once loved. I was no better than her legions of followers, all of whom I now lumped into the "idiot" category—a result of my unique form of job burnout. I was no better than they were, "wordsmith" or not.

Then again, my cyber-bullying post *was* awesome.

Those creepy Skool ghouls and their content managers must have let it through because they loved it, too. 'Cause let's face it, it was brilliant

What really pissed me off: I'd explicitly told her to contact Alex directly if she wished to discontinue our arrangement. How difficult could that have been? Instead she cc's her powerful parents and their powerful friends as well as her new bosses—whom, I might add, are not only powerful but potentially evil.

Was I the only one aside from stoned web-based conspiracy theorists who suspected the Skools were too good to be true? That their philanthropy was just a little too self-aggrandizing, that their media moves were just a little too shrewd (i.e., turning

Little White Lies into a TV show)? And yes, I do sometimes stereotype without apology: they looked like Nazis.

Ever since Coretta's confession had appeared in my inbox, and after getting axed by Alex, I'd been living in fear. The Skool twins knew they'd been duped and that I was responsible. But the show was still happening. Boldface pronouncements from the TRUTH Brigade flashed across my monitors with greater and greater frequency. It was starting to make me queasy. Yet Coretta's reputation was blemish free.

By this point I had to consider that Coretta may have been in the clear after all. And maybe I could get back to my old life.

Or better yet, maybe I could get a life.

Pink Floyd's "Money" startled me from my wistful stupor. The toothy grin of Tony Robbins lit up the communications table. I pressed SPEAKER and leaned back on BSB, drifting back into somnambulism.

"Hello," I yawned toward the phone.

"Don't try that somnambulist shit with me," Alex snapped. "And this time take me off speakerphone. I mean it."

I sat up, tapped out of speaker, and brought R$$P to my face. Then I poured on the most syrupy Errol Flynn I could muster. "Alex, so good to hear from you. To what do I owe the pleasure?"

Alex was breathless. "*Little White Lies LIVE* is on in five minutes."

"So?"

"So we need to watch it."

"Last I checked, I was off the team."

"Listen, Karl, I really don't have time for a pity party right now. And neither do you. Go to the bathroom and do whatever you need to do to wake yourself up." There was a nervousness and urgency in her voice that I hadn't heard since college. "And then I need you to be in front of that screen and back on the phone with me by eight P.M."

"Okay. Okay. I got it. I'm wide awake. And I don't need to go to the bathroom."

"Good."

"Alex, what's going on?"

"Just put on Pulse TV."

"It's on. Now can you please tell me what this is about?"

"You'll find out soon enough. And it's going to be big. I just got off the phone with the Skool twins, and I assured them you'd be watching."

"I really don't see what this has to do with—"

"Shhhhh!"

I stared at my screen as the giant purple Pulse TV logo disappeared to reveal a presumably live shot of the PULSE TV LIVE New York studio.

The simple set consisted of a giant continuous video screen—curved at the bottom in a soft right angle. It served as both the backdrop and the stage itself. It flashed from solid black to solid white, back and forth in rapid succession, like a giant strobe light. Then the set went black for a split second as a pulsating hip-hop beat kicked in, joined by a bass line reminiscent of the *Barney Miller** and *Night Court** theme songs. The set morphed into a rapid-fire series of black-and-white patterns that got increasingly more psychedelic.

For a moment I forgot I was still on the phone with Alex until she interjected, "What an obnoxious intro."

"Trippindicular," was the only reply I could manage.

When I was on the verge of a seizure, the music halted and the screen turned to black. The set lit up again, and there she was.

Coretta White, dressed in a little black dress with tiny white polka dots cut just above the knee and a black cardigan sweater. Oh, and black combat boots. She wore an uncertain smile. Her hair rested on her shoulders in loose, bouncy curls. The screen behind and beneath her glowed an eerie blood red.

"Oh my God," Alex whispered in my ear. "She looks amazing."

It was true. She was stunning. But at the same time, she looked a bit stunned. I could tell she felt out of place in the midst of all that media technology. It was weird. Even though we had never met in person, I felt as if I was seeing her again after a long absence. Still not the real thing, but certainly more real than the name behind a blog, a voice on the phone, a Gchat buddy, or a face flashing by on the side of a bus.

Watching her now, standing alone on that ridiculous bad-trip Möbius soundstage, I was looking upon Coretta for the first time as a fellow human being. All my feelings of ill will melted away. They were replaced by a confusing and scary mixture of pride, envy, and sympathetic stage fright.

Single white words began to scroll up and across the black screen, starting on the floor in front of Coretta, vanishing at the top of my monitor:

LITTLE

WHITE

LIES

TRUTH

HONOR

JUSTICE

RESPECT

ETHICS

Coretta stood quietly, waiting for the applause of the studio audience to die down. Once the crowd had settled, she addressed the cameras and began reading from the teleprompter.

The words scrolling up the screen matched up with what Coretta was reading: "Good evening. And welcome to the premiere of *Little White Lies LIVE*. I'm your host, Coretta White. Thank you for joining me tonight as we embark on this epic journey in search of the TRUTH."

The scrolling subtitles struck me as an odd choice, especially with such a trite mission statement. I sighed, and Alex shushed me again.

That's when the words began to change.

"Oh, shit." My jaw dropped as I saw what was happening. "The email."

Coretta stopped reading and whirled around at the all-encompassing stage-set screen, which now glowed a pale parchment yellow, with lines of bold black Courier font moving past her from front to back.

At that moment, the Skool twins entered the stage from opposite rear corners. Karin and Anders wore matching white suits with white ties—ironically (I guessed?) dressed like attendants at the gates of Heaven. The siblings each grabbed Coretta lightly by an arm and gently turned her body to face the audience. The text scroll paused, with the first paragraph of Coretta's confessional email emblazoned against the glowing backdrop.

"Well, this is getting interesting," I deadpanned.

"You have no idea, Karl," Alex whispered. "And honestly, neither do I. Just promise me you'll keep watching, and that you'll answer your phone as soon as it rings."

"Okay. I promise."

"Good. And don't put them on speakerphone!"

"Wait! What? Who's them?"

She'd hung up. I returned my gaze from R$$P back to the large monitor and PULSE TV LIVE. Coretta was trembling.

"Don't be nervous, Coretta," Anders said. "Shall we read the letter?"

Karin laughed. She turned to the cameras while she spoke to Anders. "Anders, maybe we should explain this to our audience first . . ."

"Karin, the letter explains everything." With one hand he gestured toward the teleprompter above the camera. "Care to do the honors?"

Karin nodded, her eyes never leaving the camera. "What follows is an email we recently received, verbatim, from Miss Coretta White." She cleared her throat with a single sharp grunt and began to read Coretta's confession in a dull monotone.

Seeing Coretta trapped in that sadistic web of humiliation as they excoriated her with her own words, I didn't feel what I expected I would feel. I'd been pissed off at her, yes. But there was no schadenfreude. There was no righteousness at justice being served. Instead there was horror. All I saw was a naïve teenager, suffering for no good reason. Suddenly I was engulfed with rage. I was as paralyzed as Coretta. (Except for when I winced slightly at the mention of my name.) By the time Karin reached the end of the letter, Coretta was crying. She broke free from the twins' clutches and darted from the cameras' view.

Anders and Karin exchanged Fox News–style puzzled grins.

Then Anders addressed the audience, reading a prepared statement from the teleprompter. "First of all, on behalf of Pulse TV, our board of directors, and my sister Karin—and on behalf of *Little White Lies* and Miss Coretta White—I would like to apologize to you, our viewers.

"What you've just witnessed was not easy to watch. We understand that. Nor was it easy for us to present such a spectacle. But it was wholly necessary for us to clear the air and clarify our vision for the show before we can proceed with *Little White Lies*.

"This is a show founded on the principles of truth, honor, justice, and respect. And lastly, *ethics*. Our original host clearly violated those principles long before this show became a reality. *Little White Lies* cannot and will not abide frauds, imposters, liars, and the like. That is, unless we can find a host who has consciously chosen to embrace such an identity and all its attending foibles."

Karin registered scripted surprise at Anders. "Wait a minute. Are you saying . . . ?"

"I am." Anders nonchalantly pulled an iPhone from his pocket. "I say we give him a call right now."

Karin smiled mischievously and turned to the audience. "Why not?"

Anders began dialing, and Karin buried her face in her hands for dramatic effect. It conjured about as much emotion as one might expect from a wooden puppet. It embodied exactly none of the principles they'd just listed.

I'd almost forgotten where I was. I almost felt like I was *there*, with her.

As Anders started pressing numbers, the touch tones became audible to the audience. Then Pink Floyd kicked in. Not on Pulse TV, in my apartment. Tony Robbins smiled from his post on the communications table. I reached for R$$P. I slid my finger to answer the call and instinctively engaged the speakerphone. A garble of feedback bounced from my computer speakers, causing me to lunge for the mute button on my keyboard. "Hello." I tried to sound as wide awake as possible.

"Hello," Anders replied. I gazed into his ice-blue eyes as he greeted me from the set of *Little White Lies*. There was an odd delay, maybe a second or two, between the movement of his lips and his voice in my ear.

It felt as if he could see me, too, even though I knew he couldn't. "Is this Karl Ristoff, the real and genuine voice behind the *Little White Lies* blog?"

"This is Karl," I replied simply.

Two seconds passed before onscreen Anders heard the answer.

"Well, Karl," he finally asked with a shit-eating grin, "how would *you* like to host your own TV show?"

CHAPTER THIRTEEN

Coretta (March 15–18, 2014)

As I stood in front of the cameras, sandwiched between these Antichrist twins, I knew only one thing: nobody could help me.

My escape from the set was a blur. Within seconds, I found myself spilling into the never-ending chaos of Times Square. I felt like I was in Tokyo or something. All of the lights, all of the noises—it seemed like everyone was speaking a different language. I couldn't breathe. As I hustled down the street, I clutched my purse. I was afraid to look at my phone. I didn't want anyone to call me, or text me, or—OH GOD—leave a voicemail.

Soon I was on the subway platform, relieved to be underground. I stood staring at the tracks, and while I wasn't really thinking of killing myself, I'd be lying if I said the thought of jumping in front of the next train didn't cross my mind.

You really want the truth as to why I didn't? The TRUTH? I didn't want to ruin the cutest outfit I'd worn in a long time, especially not my brand-new Steve Madden combat boots. (And now you can shut up.)

Nobody was home when I arrived. My parents were still trying to find me, in or around what had become the ground zero of my former self. I couldn't text them to say I was okay. I was beyond mortified, beyond humiliated; I was at a point where I wished I could simply erase my existence.

I curled up on my bed, in all my clothes, and pulled the covers over my face, as if that would provide a buffer against the blanket of shame that smothered me. While the shame was familiar, it was also different, more panic-inducing.

I had been scared of what would happen if everyone found out. That's why I wrote the letter. This time, there was nothing I could do to escape.

All I could do was cry. Cry and wait to hear what people had to say about me, and what I did, and how I let them down. I guess I deserved it. This was the price I had to pay for thinking I could cheat the system.

In the two days since Rome (my life) fell, I didn't leave my room for anything but a bodily function. While most people probably thought it was simply because I couldn't bear the thought of people looking at me, I was actually sick. I had a fever, headache, chills, plus a series of nightmares that would make *American Horror Story* look like *Dora the Explorer*: the Skool twins, Karl, my parents, Mike, Mike's parents, and Tokyo, all somehow tied to *Little White Lies*.

The Tokyo part is a bit confusing to me as well, but I think it's because of the Times Square lights . . . You get it.

My parents knew that I needed my space. Still, the day after the show, they did make me listen to a brief lecture. I had to hand it to them: they kept it under five minutes. And they let me stay in bed. I didn't really even listen. The specifics didn't matter. They sat on the edge of my mattress and expressed general disappointment. They acknowledged that I likely had enough regret to last an eternity and reminded me that I shouldn't give up on myself.

Mostly I wondered why they weren't yelling. I almost felt worse because they were so quiet. There was a sadness in their eyes that I hadn't seen since we went to my grandfather's funeral when I was eleven. And it occurred to me that I'd never again see that glazed joy I'd started to take for granted, that had annoyed me so much. Ever.

The next morning—realizing that I'd lived through wanting to jump out the window as my parents periodically appeared in my room to sit on my bed and squeeze my feet as a measure of support—I somehow mustered the courage to turn my phone back on. *Lord Jesus*, I had fifty text messages.

Only three voicemails, though. I decided to tackle the voicemails first.

Mike Cornelius (Mobile), Yesterday, 45 seconds:

"Hey, Coretta, it's Mike. I mean, you know that, because you're seeing my name, and hearing my voice. But ummm . . . yeah, I would've done this in person, but your parents say you're sick, and by the way I hope you feel better, and I would've called you. Well, I am calling you, but you're not picking up. Anyways, I know you have a lot on your plate, and I do still think you're a good person who wants to do the right thing, but . . . ummm . . . yeah, I think that we should stop seeing each other for a while. This really is hard for me, Coretta, and I don't want you to think I'm abandoning you, but I just really need to take some time, and I think you do,

too. Oh, and you don't need to call me back. Just focus
on you right now. Okay, take care. Bye.

Well, some might have classified that as a tough pill to
swallow.

As I listened to Mike's words, I closed my eyes. I felt as if
I was back on the train platform, staring at my freshly shined
combat boots. The worst part of Mike breaking up with me
wasn't even that I liked him so much—and in fact, had grown
to like him more than ever—and would really miss him. It
wasn't that he wouldn't kiss me again, that he wouldn't
be waiting at my locker in the mornings, that he would no
longer look at me with that pride he had when he first heard
about *Little White Lies*. No, the worst part was that I knew
he didn't really have a choice. I'd humiliated his entire family.
I wouldn't go out with me anymore, either.

Next, a voicemail from Skool 1. Hadn't they had enough
fun kicking me while I was down, and, ahem, on national
television? Did they really need to call and leave a voicemail?

KARIN or ANDERS SKOOL, I don't know which
(mobile), 55 seconds:

"Hello, Coretta, it is Karin and Anders. Karin speaking
right now. We really are so sorry about how things had
to happen the other night. Our network is founded on
certain principles, and while we wanted to believe that
protecting you fell under that rubric—while uncomfortable—we came to the conclusion that it would be both
legally and ethically compromising.

"Anders speaking now. Coretta, per your contract,
you are no longer allowed on the premises of Pulse TV

Inc. And while I wish you well, and this may be painful to hear, we own the name and branding concept for *Little White Lies*. I'm sure your parents' lawyers have filled you in, but: you violate your contract; we retain the rights. So sorry about that, truly. You will receive one check for the first show. Even though you walked off set, we still feel that you should get paid for that. Finally, we both want to add: You are so bright and talented and young, and we know that you will have many successes. This is a bump in your road. Cheers."

Well, that was as expected. Incredibly disheartening and laced with intrinsic evil, yes, but as expected. Lucky for them, simply reading the words "Little White Lies" made me want to vomit, so having them usurp my brand wasn't as devastating as you might imagine. And they always sounded overly polished and rehearsed.

Besides, I was taking quite a bit of NyQuil.

But that voicemail was more unsettling even than the mental imagery I had burned into my brain of those two in the white suits, white ties, and their translucent hair. I mean, seriously, who does that?

The third voicemail was from a number I didn't recognize. I guess if I lived through the first two, I could take another hit.

(212) 555-7367 (UNKNOWN) 40 seconds:

"Hi, Coretta, it's Esther Cornelius, Michael's mother. I just wanted to let you know that you could've come to us if you needed help. You really put us in a compromising spot by having us vouch for you. The Skool twins are such good people, and you put them in a terrible position. I know you're probably aware of all of this, but I just needed to say that, and I probably shouldn't be leaving this voicemail, but I know you're better than this. You'll learn from this, Coretta, if you really want to. Take care."

Esther Cornelius was someone I truly, really, honestly *admired*—unlike anyone else involved in this whole fiasco. So hearing her ramble, her voice cracking the entire time, was in some ways even harder than having to hear her son break up with me via voicemail. I'd let her down that much? She cared about me enough to cry about all of this? I'd only had dinner at their house once! Was there no rest for the weary? How much more of this could I take?

My Facebook had 212 personal messages, mostly from outraged strangers, and most too obscene or disturbed to make me feel threatened. Reading their posts, it would be safe to assume that I murdered their family members or threw their pets into oncoming traffic.

Then there were the Google Alerts. My name kept popping up in some new story on some different website. The Skool twins were doing their best to drag my name through the mud, set it on fire, and then put it on a cross in the town square that is the Internet.

I was no longer able to log in on Twitter as @LittleWhite-Lies, but I had a look at the feed anyway. My number of followers had been cut in half; I wasn't sure if I'd been deserted for being a phony, or if these un-followers withdrew their support from the show because of my ousting. Maybe the mass exodus was more due to the latter, but I more suspected the former. I didn't risk reading any of the actual tweets.

There *were* a handful of people that messaged me privately to say that everyone messes up, and that I should keep my head up and yada yada, but a small number. Insignificant. Okay, exactly three people, all of whom had less than ten followers on any social media platform. Combined.

The general message was loud and clear: I was now one of those people you had to hate. You'd be missing out if you *didn't* hate me.

Day three after the Chernobyl of my life, I was still sick but thinking more clearly. Perhaps it was that I was taking less NyQuil, but I also had some questions.

I started to wonder how Rachel's parents knew Alex Melrose.

I know it's not cute to try to deflect responsibility from oneself, but I never would've gotten into this specific mess without Rachel introducing me to Alex and her services.

That very afternoon, seventy-two hours after the Pulse TV *Hindenburg*, Rachie-Rach texted me:

> Hey- I want you to know I'm thinking about you, but I know how you are and want to give you some space. When you want to talk, please call me. I love you. I ruff you. You know this. We will get through this ☺

I called her immediately.

"Hey, Coretta!"

"Hey, Rach." My voice sounded weird. Hoarse and gravelly. Maybe because I hadn't used it in three days.

"I'm so glad you called, Coretta. I've been really worried

about you." She spoke even more quickly than usual. "I made sure all of the teachers emailed you your homework assignments."

"Thanks for that. I'm kind of glad that I'm sick. Everyone at school must be talking about me. Right? Hello, are they talking about me?"

"No! I mean, yes, of course they are, but it's high school. Who cares? Everyone is talking about everyone all the time. Hey, I heard that Mike broke up with you. I imagine that combined with . . . well, everything else . . . I'm sorry."

"I've definitely seen better times, Rach. Yeah, I can't blame Mike right now. That said, I am still feeling like he threw the baby out with the bathwater."

"What?! You're pregnant? You had an abortion? What?"

"No, it's an expression. You know, throwing the baby out with the bathwater?" (Every time Rachel didn't know a common phrase like this—often—I felt like I should explain it to her, and then I would instantly regret it. She had a 31 ACT score, I mean, come on.) "Rachel! It's saying you're giving up on everything when one thing goes wrong. Never mind, that's not why I called. It's just . . . all of a sudden it occurred to me that I don't know how your parents know Alex Melrose. I bet my own parents are wondering, too. You just told me to trust you, and the next thing I know, I'm Gchatting Karl Ristoff. And I'm not blaming you or your parents or anyone. I'm just trying to make sense of this shit salad that I've created."

Rachel didn't answer right away. Silence hung between us.

"Everyone has secrets," she finally said. "Everyone needs catering to every once in a while."

"That's a very vague answer, Rach. I need *concrete* answers. To questions like, did you ever think about who is paying Alex? Or who is paying Karl? How did your parents know to call her? Do we even know who she really is? Because I know I don't really know who Karl is, and I just think that the way everything came into play was a little too well-played—"

"Coretta," Rachel interrupted, "you know that this is coming from me as a friend, okay? I think you just really need to focus on putting this all behind you."

Have you ever had something go down between yourself and someone you trust? And then the next time you talk, that person looks at you or talks to you like you've never met? It's a terrible feeling, and I heard it in Rachel's voice.

"Stop bullshitting me, Rach," I said. Because why not?

She sniffed. "Coretta, believe me, I'm sorry that this all played out this way. I really wish I could make it all go away, but trust me; I think that we should just move on. Okay? Coretta? Are you there?"

I sat in silence on the other end.

Should we move on, Rachel? Should *we*? Where did Rachel get off using the term *we*? She was not on this sinking ship with me. She asked me to trust her: she set me up with someone who could assist me in being the captain of my ship, and that cocaptain and I ended up lighting the ship on fire. Now that ship was at the bottom of the ocean. It was not *our* ship. It was *my* ship—and my skipper Karl's. True to form, like a good captain, I sank with my vessel.

CHAPTER FOURTEEN

Karl (March 15–29, 2014)

When someone offers you your own TV show—even if that someone has just publicly humiliated and destroyed the reputation of a person you care about, even if that someone likely wants to destroy you, too—you accept the offer.

More specifically, if this offer is made via telephone during a live TV broadcast (immediately after the aforementioned character assassination) you answer with an exuberant "Oh, *HELL*, yes!"

Then you literally kiss your iPhone, inadvertently ending the call, and you guzzle the remainder of your beer.

Then, because you've already been drinking heavily for more consecutive weeks than you care to remember, you crack open another.

You tell yourself you're celebrating. Half of the beer gushes all over your floor. You are toasting your new success with the only person who really matters—you. But you know at a deeper level that you are pounding down cartoonish amounts of alcohol for a very different reason.

That reason is simple. Fear.

When the phone rings again—long after Pulse TV has replaced what was supposed to be the debut of teen sensation

Coretta White's *Little White Lies* with a very long infomercial about SKOOLS 4 ALL—you're three sheets to the wind. You've forgotten your fear. Or at least buried it. Lowercased it. Which is easy when the shovel is the Skool twins' promise of a Mercedes limo bus (pronounced "boose") waiting outside your door.

I left my apartment with my two phones and the clothes on my body and walked unsteadily to the waiting Mercedes limo "boose."

It was more like a limo van. But less creepy sounding. "Limo van" sounds like a high-class rape wagon. "Limo bus" sounds like a giant limousine full of wealthy old people. At least to me, it does.

This limo bus was virtually empty, except for an attractive young woman wearing a gray skirt and purple blouse, with blonde hair several shades darker than that of the Skools. Her outfit and demeanor suggested a cross between paralegal and flight attendant. The limo was like a dance club right before it opens. My own private disco, with a wraparound leather bench, hypnotic floor-to-ceiling LED lighting, a fully stocked bar, and the requisite flatscreen TV emblazoned with the Pulse TV logo. "Juicy" by Biggie Smalls blasted from the sound system. It had the comforting effect that some clever Belgian had likely anticipated.

Kudos, Karin and Anders, I thought with a silly smile.

"Mr. Ristoff, welcome to Pulse TV!" the woman said. Her accent was ambiguously French. "Please have a seat. My name is Chloe, and I'm here to make your ride to company headquarters as comfortable as possible. Would you care for a drink?"

I sank into the cushy couch at the back. "Gin and juice?"

"*C'est bon!* Gin *et* juice. Like Snoop Dogg."

I have to say, hearing a beautiful woman with an ambiguously French accent name-check Uncle Snoop made me feel pretty great.

That was the last I saw of Chloe for quite some time.

And then I woke up.

Or did I? Was I still dreaming?

Turns out I did wake up, but these questions were consistent with the night before and the weeks that would follow. This phase of my life quickly became more and more dreamlike. And by dreamlike, I mean confusing, hyperbolic, surreal, amazing, terrifying, and beyond reason. Oh, and quite blurry; I remembered very little of it.

"Good morning, Karl! How are you feeling today?"

I opened my eyes at the sound of newly familiar voices speaking in unison. First I noticed that I wasn't home, and that the bedding was exceptionally fine. I had no time to guesstimate the thread count, since I next noticed that the Skool twins were addressing me from a large flatscreen positioned just above the foot of this strange bed.

Okaaaay. . . . *Creepy.*

I rubbed my eyes and sat up. The shock of being awakened by the smiling faces of my new employers—appearing like two overeager morning newscasters—overcame my total lack of recollection of going, or being put, to bed. (Not to mention undressing). These sensations contributed to my confusion as to whether I was awake or asleep, conscious or dreaming, alive or dead, in heaven or hell. Or purgatory . . .

Looking back, it feels like all of the above.

"Hey, Skools!" I surprised myself at how chipper I sounded. "Top of the morning to you. Where *are* you, anyway? Your resolution is phenomenal. And by the way, where am I?"

"You are in your new home, Karl," Karin assured me, smiling.

Thankfully she and Anders had changed out of their white suits. They were now wearing coordinated ensembles more closely resembling casual business attire, or morning newscaster attire, the *Morning Joe* variety. Karin wore a crisp white blouse with the collar popped. The top buttons were undone to show a large purple stone vaguely shaped like Africa, set in gold, hanging just below her neck by a chunky yet elegant flat gold chain. Anders wore his crisp white shirt with a shimmering purple necktie, contained in a well-fitting navy blazer.

Of course, I could only see them from the chest up.

"Williamsburg, Karl," Anders added. "A very hip neighborhood, as you well know. And you are twenty-six floors above it all, with sweeping views of the East River and Manhattan."

"And where are you guys?" I asked casually, trying to hide my discomfort.

"We are at work, Karl, *of course*." Karin conjured a clumsy smile, perhaps to cover up her bitchy *of course*, adding, "In the video conference room."

Anders jumped in. "But we do not expect *you* to be at work today. It is a Sunday, Karl. Enjoy it! Besides, we had a very productive night last night—in addition to the celebrating!"

I rifled through fuzzy memory files, searching for some shred of recollection that might pertain to productivity. All I could come up with was a disturbing dream fragment that had me signing with my own blood what I vaguely recalled was a contract of eternal servitude. I remembered thinking during the dream how difficult it was to sign my name with my bloody left pinky.

"So are there more cameras installed in this condo, or just this one I'm looking at now?"

Both twins laughed. "These cameras will be an excellent source of potential content for the show, Karl," Anders said. "This was your idea, of course."

"*My* idea?!" I gasped, pulling the covers over my face.

"Perhaps we have called a bit too early, Anders," Karin interjected with a wink in her voice. "I think Karl could benefit from a bit more rest, and perhaps some time to explore his new home . . . and to consider this exciting new opportunity that lies ahead."

The screen faded to black.

I fell back against the soft pillows and desperately tried to repossess some small scrap of memory from the preceding night.

And then it occurred to me: in spite of a lifelong personal pact vowing never to do such a thing, I'd just had my first video chat.

I spent the rest of the day exploring my new home and exploiting its many amenities. The view of Manhattan across the East River was indeed spectacular. I felt like I could reach out and touch the tip of the Empire State Building. I couldn't wait for it to get dark so I could see what color they would light it tonight—something very New York that I had never cared about before.

I selected a pod of French roast from the prodigious supply and made myself an espresso with the fancy Italian machine. The fridge was stocked. So was the bar. I added some Baileys to my latte and ran a bath in the raised Jacuzzi tub.

All the while I was on the hunt for hidden surveillance cameras, finding them throughout the spacious one-bedroom spread. I determined that these tiny, unobtrusive lenses covered every basic angle in each room, including the bathroom. Nothing would transpire in this apartment without being recorded.

So be it.

Later, as I took a bubble bath, I began to make a mental list of priorities:

1. Live it up
2. Take no prisoners
3. Party my ass off
4. Make television history

Number four was tricky. I knew what the show *shouldn't* be. There was no point in satirizing blowhards like Sean Hannity and Bill O'Reilly, because Stephen Colbert had already taken care of that perfectly. Besides, I wanted to dig deeper. I wanted to open up myself to the world. (Given all the cameras, I had no choice.) And I wanted to open up the world to what was really going on in the world.

Here in the big bathtub, I couldn't help but think *big*. My smile no longer masked a hangover; it became genuine. I didn't want to be like Rachel Maddow or those other know-it-alls from MSNBC. Anyway, ever since I'd witnessed Russell Brand eviscerate the entire cast of *Morning Joe* in 2013 (ending the segment by calling Mika a "shaft grasper"; seriously, YouTube it!), I couldn't even watch them for my morning shits and giggles anymore.

Now that I thought about it, Russell Brand wasn't a bad role model. But I was never going to be that thin, handsome, or British—despite my Erroll Flynn affectations. Most important, I didn't have a legion of fans.

Strange. And ironic. In a lot of ways, I was just like Coretta. But without the youth, beauty, or powerful parents.

I wasn't smiling anymore.

It didn't matter. I was having an epiphany. Yes, it was during this dreamy bubble bath that I begrudgingly admitted to myself, *I already have the perfect role model.* And that was Coretta herself. Or rather, the Coretta White I'd deluded myself into believing I knew. The best way to honor Coretta was to make my initial image of her (however false) a reality.

But the so-called "lies" of her parents were very pale indeed (pun intended) when compared to the BIG FAT LIES that have been passed off by the RICH WHITE MALE ruling class of this great nation since its inception.

Those were the lies I wanted to explore: REAL WHITE LIES.

So my first order of business would be to change the name of the show.

My next pressing question—perhaps easier to address than the previous ones—was whether or not I should use the show as a platform (finally!) to promote my rap career.

I knew what Alex would say. But that was *her* problem.

Monday morning I felt like a badass striding through the Pulse TV offices (had I been here before?) in my all-black ensemble fresh from Barneys in Brooklyn—care of a black titanium Amex card that had mysteriously appeared on my pillow during my bubble bath. I noted the deferential silence I created with my black ensemble, walking amongst the blond interns in their white Oxford shirts and the twenty-somethings in their hoodies.

When I reached the glass-enclosed conference room, the Skools welcomed me with cheery bemusement.

Strange—they looked both thinner and taller in real life.

"Ahhh, the man in black!" Anders exclaimed. I wondered if he realized he was making a Johnny Cash* reference.

Karin eyed me up and down and up again. "Very chic, Karl. And so confident! I like this new look for you. You already appear successful. And those pants are such a great fit. Black denims, very, very nice."

"I should hope so! These jeans were eight hundred bucks!" I half expected at least one raised eyebrow at a pair of pants that cost twenty times more than any I had purchased before in my life.

They were unruffled.

I didn't see the point in adding that my simple black button-down shirt cost $575 and that my John Varvatos* boots were over $1400, or that I had bought two pairs, and five identical jeans-and-shirt combos.

I had never shopped this way before, but I felt compelled to blow as much money as possible as quickly as possible. I had considered inviting my three best subcontract-tweeters— Bodhi, Sarah, and Kris—to dinner, with the intention of offering them jobs on the show, but decided against it for now. Baby steps.

Sitting with the Skools at the conference table were three white-shirt interns. Oh, and Ethan, their teeny assistant.

I wasn't nervous per se, but I was definitely on edge. I was navigating the unknown, and I had no clue about what was real and what wasn't. I'd gone from weeks of being cooped up in my basement hovel, living off YouTube and takeout, to waking up in a luxury high-rise apartment with unlimited credit and my own TV show. Needless to say, *this* didn't feel real. The problem was that I couldn't recall anything else in my life that felt "real," either.

"So glad to have you here," Anders said, his tone now formal. "Coffee? So nice to have you back after your contract signing."

"Yes, please." *Contract signing?*

"Milk, two sugars?" Anders asked. "No Baileys, I'm afraid."

"Yes, how did . . . ?" Then I remembered. *Cameras.*

Ethan rose from his seat and vaulted to the coffee maker in the corner of the room. He gently set my coffee in front of me with a subservient nod. Karin gestured toward the three white-shirts. "Also joining us this morning is Emma, who will be your—how did you put it?—*daysistant*; as well as Sander, your *nightsistant*, and Wannes, who will be your *scrivener*."

I gave each new member of my staff a friendly nod as I took a sip of my coffee. I now realized my mug was the only one on the table. I frantically tried to recall any shred of a contract signing. I couldn't.

Deliberately or not, Anders addressed my confusion. "Contract *negotiations* was more like it, ha, ha. You are a pretty tough dealmaker, Mr. Ristoff. And we were a bit surprised to have you insist on 'absolute creative control'—especially as you have no experience producing a television program. But when you said it was a deal *breaker*, well, we had to say yes."

I forced a smile. "How did you get the credit card issued so quickly? I mean, you didn't even offer me the job until Saturday night . . ."

"One of the advantages of owning several banks, Karl."

I was still blanking out on this purported contract session, but I had to admit that demanding "absolute creative control" did sound like something I would demand after double-digit beers. And for as long as I could remember, I had wanted my own "scrivener"—basically a personal scribe to jot down all the brilliant shit I say all day to record it for posterity. I imagined that *daysistant* and *nightsistant* sounded like my own slurred pronunciations of "day assistant" and "night assistant." So maybe things weren't going so terribly after all . . .

"Well, I do appreciate you meeting my demands. And I'd love to help you put these clearly capable interns to good use." I made a point of talking equally to Anders and Karin, which relieved me of holding eye contact with either one of them for too long. "But I had the intention to hire some people from my circle to fill out my writing staff and to work in production."

The Skools' smiles simultaneously disappeared.

"I'm afraid that won't be possible," Karin replied.

"But . . . didn't you just say I have absolute creative control?"

"I'm afraid the hiring of staff is a *personnel* decision, not a creative decision," Anders offered by way of explanation. "Karl, we went over this on Saturday. We are already taking quite a large risk by putting you at the helm of this television program. We can't take chances with outsiders on your staff."

"Understood," I replied.

Across the table, all smiles returned. "Now, Karl," Karin said, "you had so many great ideas on Saturday. I loved your 'White Men *Can* Rap' concept. It is so—what is the word?— dope!"

Horror returned. I slurped some coffee and set the mug down quickly. "Well, that is certainly something to consider." I slouched in an effort to portray effortless confidence. "But my first order of creative business is this: I want to change the name of the show."

I hesitated. I expected disapproval. Instead, everyone at the table leaned toward me with eyes full of interest.

"How about this?" I raised my eyebrows and pointed friendly finger-guns at Karin and Anders. "*Real. White. Lies.*"

Nobody responded. Everyone seemed to be holding their breath.

I took another hasty sip of coffee. "I'm talking about the lies that the military-industrial complex shoves down the throats of poor people. But funny."

Karin shot a smile at her twin. "I like what I am hearing, Karl," she said, "You are brimming with so many great ideas and concepts. So radical, so passionate. And the new title is brilliant. Anders and I have decided to delay your debut for one more week, so that you and your staff will have adequate time to develop the best show possible."

Anders nodded. "Keep thinking, Karl," he said. He glanced at his phone, signaling our meeting was over. "We will meet again tomorrow morning to discuss our progress. And by all means, have some fun tonight!"

I did have fun that night. I also had fun during the next two weeks: a fuzzy blur that involved zero preparation leading up to the premier of *Real White Lies*.

I also googled myself more than ever:

Karl Ristoff	Q

Old white ghost-tweeter replaces young black tv host . . .

Karl Ristoff becomes the white in little white lies . . .

Coretta White loses tv job to ghost-blogger . . .

Karl Ristoff: man of mystery — soon to be history? . . .

Now I saw the benefits of never having set up a proper Facebook page. There were no old embarrassing photos of me for public consumption—that is, unless you consider my driver's license photo and my high school yearbook photos to be embarrassing, which they kind of were.

It seemed that the blogosphere was on a massive hunt to locate recent photos of Pulse TV's newest star.

But I had a show to create. And partying to do. I also charged two of my top subcontract-tweeters—Kris and Sarah—with conducting opposition research on my new bosses, the Skool twins.

Alex would tell me nothing. In fact, she'd stopped returning my phone calls and texts. Maybe she was pissed I'd entered into an agreement with the Skool twins without consulting her first. Or maybe once again, like at those Peter O'Toole Society shows decades ago, she was just embarrassed to be associated with me.

I couldn't blame her. The public record was rife with evidence of my misbehavior. Every morning there was an item on Page Six of the *New York Post* about my misconduct from the night before. TMZ had a fresh Karl Ristoff video nearly every day. In turn, my appearances there generated invitations to outrageous parties and exclusive nightclubs I had never imagined, even during my days of celebrity ghost-tweeting. The cycle of nighttime naughtiness was the perfect promotional storm for the debut of *Real White Lies*.

The show itself, however, did not look so promising.

Despite my guarantee of "creative control" over my own TV show, nothing quite came together. Prospective guests were rejected because of "booking issues" that I was assured had "nothing whatsoever to do with the direction." A few were deemed "antithetical to the interests of our sponsors." Somehow "creative control" meant I had the power to think up any idea I wanted for the show, but with no actual mechanism to help me bring these ideas to fruition.

And then, all of a sudden it seemed, came the big night.

I did have one big pre-show success; I secured the rights for my choice of theme song. It was "Lies," performed by the cartoon character Baby Cakes from animator Brad Neely's *China, IL* series on Adult Swim. But even in the countdown to showtime, it didn't bring me much pleasure. (Granted, I was hungover. Again.) When the cheap Casio drum beat came to a halting stop and the soundstage went dark, I wondered for the hundred-thousandth time: *What the hell am I doing? Who am I? What am I?*

For once, the questions were pertinent. Masses of people were wondering the same things. Too bad I still had no answer. I stationed myself atop the same wack-ass concave video soundstage on which Coretta had met her televised demise just two weeks prior.

Déjà fucking vu.

I was wearing my new rock star uniform—black button-down shirt, black denim jeans, outrageously expensive boots that looked like they might have been pulled from a sleeping hobo's feet. Think Trent Reznor* wannabe. Not what I was going for; it's just where my "look" ended up. Maybe *that's* who and what I was, someone who just "ended up" with things—a look, a show, whatever, all wrong.

When the music ended, the stage glowed a yellowish-white. Now I was backlit and bottom-lit so that I initially appeared like a silhouette.

I'd prepared for this part, of course; I wasn't winging it completely. We'd gone through a full dress rehearsal yesterday. But still, winging it was what it felt like.

"Good evening," I said to the cameras and bright lights. My voice boomed from the invisible mic clipped to my shirt. "I'm Karl. Welcome to *Real White Lies*."

That's when the scripted portion of the evening ended. At least according to the script that we had followed yesterday. The house went black again. All at once I was hit with six consecutive blasts from a powerful spotlight. I cringed, momentarily blinded. Again the house went dark as eerie guttural bass tones hummed from the sound system, vibrating inside my abdomen.

"A little something different for you folks at home," I lamely quipped, trying to recover. My voice was inaudible. Of course it was. My mic had been shut off.

The stage glowed once more, below and behind me, and I heard a collective gasp from the small studio audience. I turned to see a giant projection of buck-naked Karl Ristoff (thankfully with pixilated privates) holding a bottle of tequila and singing—poorly—an ancient megahit by Nelly: "It's Getting Hot in Herrrre."

The camera angle changed to reveal two uniformed NYPD officers, one male and one female, both unimpressed.

You can imagine what followed.

In case you can't, I'll spell it out in excruciating detail.

First a quick montage of me in various stages of undress at my "new home," accompanied by generic circus music. I had no memory of any of it. Then came embarrassing shots from my oeuvre of low-budget rap videos: MC Expensive Meal draped with bacon; MCEM being straddled by an

Amy Winehouse lookalike; MCEM fighting over Viagra in an old folks' home and then creeping through the bedrooms.

The videos had seemed innocent and funny when I'd made them.

In this context, however, I looked like an out of control idiot.

When the video ended, the stage glowed red, and the regular stage lights came up in front of me. I heard Anders before I saw him.

"And these are just the highlights, ladies and gentlemen," he announced gleefully. I didn't need to spot Karin to know that the Skool twins were repeating the flanking maneuver they'd pulled with Coretta. Soon enough they were at my side, each placing a gentle hand on a respective elbow.

I jerked away and crossed my arms in defiance. I stared directly into the camera, trying to muster as much self-confidence as possible. Mostly I was trying not to cry on TV. I knew there was nothing I could say, even if I did have a live microphone. And any attempt to snatch a mic from the Skools—any physical outburst—would only make me look like more of a fool.

So I listened.

Or pretended to. It was something about balancing the scales between me and Coretta . . . the importance of exposing frauds in our midst, including Coretta White, Karl Ristoff, and Alex Melrose of AllYou™, the fraudulent business that was largely responsible for this entire mess . . . the vapidity of gossip and the insanity of conspiracy theorists . . . the cancellation of *Real White Lies* (duh) and the announcement of a brand-new program to take its place—devoted to their SKOOLS 4 ALL initiative . . .

When they finished their public scolding/promo spiel, the lights went down.

Finally, something else I'd rehearsed for: the show had cut to commercials. The Skools attempted to escort me off the stage, offering vague apologies mixed with stern rebukes and threats of lawyers, tabloids—and most important, the police. But I knew better than to hang around and protest. I broke free and somehow found my way to the street below.

I didn't bother trying to return to my "new home." No doubt they'd already changed the locks. Instead I opted for the nearest bar, which happened to be inside a Bubba Gump Shrimp Co. I ordered a large Lt. Dan's Punch and slid my titanium Amex card over to the bartender. I had just made it to the bottom of my punch when the bartender approached me with a regretful look.

"I'm sorry, but your card's been declined," he said. He didn't sound apologetic. He sounded oddly like Bill O'Reilly. "I'm required by American Express to destroy it."

From beneath the counter, he pulled out a pair of thick bright orange rubber gloves, a large, long-neck beaker full of clear liquid, and a smaller cylindrical beaker. After he donned the gloves, he carefully poured the liquid into the smaller beaker. "Hydrofluoric acid," he stated matter-of-factly. "Sorry, this is company policy."

When he dropped my card into the beaker, it disintegrated before my eyes without so much as a fizzle. The liquid remained clear.

"That'll be fourteen dollars for the punch," he said, putting everything away. "And we do take cash. Would you like another?"

I shoved my hand into the front pocket of my expensive

jeans, pulled out my last crumpled twenty, and laid it on the bar. Then I shuffled out of Bubba Gump Shrimp Co. and headed to a bar where the bartender knew my name. At least there I'd be able to drink on credit.

Part III: Spring 2014

CHAPTER FIFTEEN

Coretta (March 29–30, 2014)

I sat in front of my computer, not knowing what to do.

I had just finished watching the livestream of Karl Ristoff's first *"Real" White Lies* (ha!). I'd just been subjected to that horror show.

Yes, I was still furious with Karl for agreeing to take over the hosting duties after I had been crucified for all to see. (I know I said I wouldn't use the word "crucify," but I couldn't resist any longer.) And yet it was still painful— *beyond* painful— to watch him suffer exactly the same fate. To explode on national television, thanks to the Skool twins.

Did I say explode? I meant implode.

It was worse for him, too. I knew that. I was seventeen years old. I was a kid who was an idiot. I could come back from this. I *would* come back from this. But Karl was old enough to be my father. He was a dude who made a living ghost-tweeting for celebrities and politicians. He used to be anonymous, but the Skool twins ruined that for him. Now there was a face to the name. I admit it: even in the midst of all of *my* self-pity, I felt bad for the guy.

I tried calling him repeatedly. He didn't pick up. I didn't know Karl well enough to know how he would handle this all, but if I were a betting woman, I wouldn't put my money on a happy ending. I texted him. I knew he had an aversion to phone conversations, but I hoped he would respond to a text.

> I know you probably don't want to talk right now, and believe me, I can completely relate, but I just wanted to check in on you and see how you're doing. I probably should have done a better job of warning you about the Skool twins. I'm sorry. We've really made quite the situation for ourselves, haven't we? ☺ Call me, K?

I stared at my phone waiting for the little ellipses to pop up. He'd always been prompt in responding. Just then, a text message from Rachel appeared.

> I'm at your door. Long story. Sorry I didn't call before.

Apparently my parents let Rachel in, because right as I was opening the door to go downstairs, she burst into my room. She slammed the door behind her and sat down on my bed, then put her head between her hands.

"Hey, Coretta, yeah, so I'm sorry I didn't tell you I was stopping over. I just—I watched Karl, and I had to get over here. I didn't know what to say . . ." Her voice was strained. She sounded as if she were about to cry. "Coretta, I've gotta be up front with you—"

"Rachel, I've had plenty of people tell me that I really shit the bed on this one, and I—"

"Shut up!" she snapped, glaring up at me. "I came here to tell you how I know Alex Melrose."

That got my attention. It was the one crucial piece of the puzzle that was missing. I nodded and sat down beside her. "I'm listening."

"My parents . . . my parents hired Alex last year to help them deal with some family issues. I don't even really know *what* she helped them with. I just know it had to do with my dad's law practice, and it was a big deal, and they were freaking out."

I stared at Rachel to see if she was telling the truth. Her face wasn't twitching. "Go on," I murmured.

"I found out about Alex only because I heard my mom on the phone with a friend who recommended Alex and AllYou™" Rachel said. "They said she was discreet and could help anyone with anything. So when you started to slack on stuff, I started to think that maybe she could help you. Then when you had your breakdown—the first one—I thought it was a good idea." She paused, unable to meet my eyes. "I paid for the whole thing, Coretta. I was going to surprise you and tell you on your eighteenth birthday. It was my early birthday present to you."

My mind raced as I pondered the implications of what she was saying. I wondered if she could ask AllYou™ for her money back. Probably not. It couldn't have been cheap, this early birthday present . . .

"Now I feel like I led you down this path of destruction," she went on. "I'm so sorry, Coretta. I don't even feel like that means anything at this point, but I am." Rachel buried her face in her hands again and wept. That verb is deliberate: She wasn't crying, she was *weeping*.

I laid my head on my friend's shoulder.

"Rach, I know you only wanted the best for me," I said. "Who else but you would do something so generous? And if my head had been a little less up my ass, I could've asked you for a life preserver. Instead, I thought I could handle the sharks on my own. All we can do is deal with the present, okay? Not your present to me; I mean the present, like, *now*."

Rachel nodded.

"Good. Because now I need you to put all of that aside, because I need your help. Are you ready? I need you to say that you are ready to help me."

She took a deep breath, sniffed, and wiped her eyes, "I am ready to help you."

"Good, because I need to find Karl Ristoff."

Rachel figured the best way to find Karl was to start with his boss. She punched Alex Melrose's number into my landline.

"Hello?" a gruff woman's voice answered.

"Hi, can I please speak with Alex?"

"Listen, if you're a reporter, I have no comment on Karl Ristoff or—"

"Alex, it's Coretta White."

A pause, then a sigh. "Look, kid, I'm really sorry about everything that has happened, but I've got my own problems right now. AllYou™ has seen better days. I'd appreciate it if you wouldn't give this number out to anybody."

"It's not that," I said quickly. "I'm not here to give you up to the media or anything. I'm calling because I need to talk to Karl, and I'm worried because I haven't heard so much as a snotty peep from him. Have you?"

She laughed sadly. "No, Karl hasn't picked up either of his stupid phones or answered any of my texts or emails. Not even when I tried to bait him."

"Ummm . . . bait him?"

"We've known each other a long time. Never mind. If Karl

hasn't changed, he should be at one of three places . . ." Her voice swelled; she suddenly started to sound confident, like Esther Cornelius. "You know, this is good. Can you meet me in front of the deli on Thirty-Second Street and Ninth Avenue at 10 P.M.?"

"Yes, but I'm bringing my friend."

"This isn't a field trip."

"Ma'am, I'm seventeen, and the friend is Rachel Bernstein. I believe you're acquainted."

"Touché. See you in one hour."

As Rachel and I approached the deli, I spotted Alex immediately. She was just as I expected her. Rail thin, long dark hair, wearing only black, and rocking three-inch Louboutins. Judging from the circles under her eyes, she hadn't been lying; she had definitely seen better days. Then again, we all had.

"Hi, Alex. I'm Coretta, and this is Rachel."

Alex looked both of us up and down. "Hello, girls," she said quietly. "You know, I don't usually meet my clients on the street at night. I guess there's a first for everything. Okay, so there is a dive bar around the corner, and that's where Karl usually goes if he's feeling particularly self-destructive."

Rachel, being Rachel, brought up the obvious. "Umm, we are minors. We can't go into a bar."

"Honey, I could bring a six-year-old into this place if I wore these shoes."

I could tell that Rachel wasn't quite sure what Alex meant by that—neither was I, honestly—but she zipped it nonetheless.

We walked up to the bar. It had a battered wooden door under a flashing red sign that read WALT'S. As we walked in, I kind of felt like the three of us were a busted knockoff of

Charlie's Angels. The place smelled of pee and beer. I wasn't sure which odor was stronger. Alex scanned the room and beelined to a rumpled, slouched figure in the corner. Rachel grabbed my hand, trying not to slip on the beer- (and pee-?) soaked floor.

"Karl," Alex hissed in his ear. "Karl, wake up. Karl, it's Alex!" She pushed back and forth on his shoulder with both of her hands until he finally came to. I placed the Karl I saw on TV next to the Karl slumped at that table, and all I can say is that TV works wonders. This dude looked like shit. His hair (what was left of it) was greased down on his scalp, which was clammy and red. He had nice clothes on, but they looked like he pulled them from a pile of dirty laundry.

A fitting introduction for us, I thought.

"Huh?" he croaked. He rubbed his beady red eyes. "What are you doing here, Alex? Haven't you done enough? *God.* Just let a man mourn the downfall of his empire." As Karl blinked, his gaze landed on Rachel and me. "What the f— Alex! Why did you bring—*Coretta* and—and . . . some other seemingly young woman to Walt's?!"

"Because they were worried about you, asshole. I'm worried about you. And news flash, suspicions confirmed. You're choosing to cope in an unhealthy way. How many beers have you even had?"

"Sorry I don't cope by means of mud masks and chakra cleansings, Little Miss Priss. Oh, and thank you so much for giving the Skool twins all the information they needed to destroy my entire life."

"I didn't tell them anything about you! Don't flatter yourself—"

"Oh, really? Then who is this alleged 'Noprah' person, huh? You can drop the nondisclosure bull—"

"Noprah? Noprah isn't real. I made her up because I know you're like a child, and you need incentives to do work you should be doing anyway. The person you are asking about is this one right here." Alex pointed to Rachel.

Karl tried his best to focus on Rachel. I could see it washing over his heavily lined face. I could see it in his scowl. This skinny, curly-haired, somewhat nerdy Jewish girl was the one who had come to Alex for help? Not possible.

Rachel must have felt compelled to say something. "Hi. This one is Rachel. Nice to meet you."

Karl turned back to Alex. "Noprah?" he spat.

"Yes, Karl—"

"Are you *kidding* me?"

Rachel and I backed off.

Alex and Karl kept bickering in a way that I've never seen adults do. Watching two forty-somethings fight in a place like this was somehow even sadder than one might imagine. They were making actual faces at each other, and I'm pretty sure they were referencing things that happened in college—maybe some of which the Skools had broadcast tonight on TV.

This had to stop.

"Excuse me! Can you two shut up?" I didn't mean to scream so loud, but it worked. The entire bar fell silent. "Can you guys let go of your baggage?" My voice dropped to a whisper. "Don't you think it's strange that the Skool twins know so much about all of us, and none of us told them anything? Who are they getting their information from? And why? Why are *we* people that they would even want to bring down? We're nobodies! If anything, they should thank me! I volunteered for their nonprofit!"

That worked. Karl and Alex fell silent, too.

"Coretta has a point," Rachel said quietly. "Not to burst

any of your egos, but you aren't exactly la crème de la crème. And you're right; it *is* weird about the nonprofit, isn't it?"

Karl's accusing bloodshot eyes turned to Alex. Alex's eyes turned to Rachel. Rachel's eyes turned to me. We all shrugged.

Rachel kept looking at me. "Not to add salt to the injury, but do you think Mike could've told them anything about you? I mean, maybe he has access to your computer or emails or I don't know . . . Aren't Mike and his parents pretty close to the Skools?"

"I mean, they don't brunch together, but his parents are on their board. I mean, we met at their fundraiser—you know that. Mike was all starry-eyed about how the Skools were 'the masters of data collection.' And how they were using that data for good. But I can't believe Mike would hurt me on purpose."

Karl jolted up from the table. "Then let's go before the turn cools!" he slurred.

We all stared at him. What did that even mean? Whatever.

I reached for my phone and pulled up Mike's contact. I stared at his little thumbnail picture. For a second, I hesitated, remembering the days when I would call or text him all the time. It felt weird to be looking at his tiny face again. But I took a deep breath and tapped the screen.

"Hey, I'm so glad you called," he answered instantly, breathlessly.

I frowned. "You are? Mike, it's Coretta, you know that right?"

"Yes, of course I know it's you. I was just about to call you."

"Wait, what?"

"I can't really get into it on the phone, but I shouldn't have defended the Skools without really knowing what I was talking about. I turned my back on you, and I am so sorry. Can you forgive me?"

"Can I . . . ?" I had a flash of that same alternate-reality hallucinatory feeling I'd experienced when the Skools first forgave me for the letter. It set off alarm bells. "Of course I forgive you. But why would I have to? Listen, Mike, I'm calling because I wanted to know more about—"

"The Skools," he interrupted. "I know. When I watched what happened to that guy Karl, I started doing some research, and I found something. Something big. We can't talk on the phone; we've gotta meet in person. My parents aren't home right now. Can you meet me here at my house? Or I can meet you?"

"Meet me?" I looked around the bar, then at Rachel and these strange middle-aged people who were suddenly a part of my life. "No, you can't meet me. My parents are home, so we can't go there."

Rachel shrugged. "Don't look at me. My family is always home," she said. "If not my parents, my bubbi will be." She jerked her shoulder toward Karl. "And this guy isn't going near there."

Alex rolled her eyes. "Tell your boyfriend we're coming over, and to try to find a nice red wine lying around the house. Let's move."

I knew that I shouldn't be excited about going to meet my ex-boyfriend. Especially not with my best friend, whom I conveniently forgot about during my rise to the top. And let's not forget accompanied by a drunk forty-something white man and a malnourished forty-something white woman. But what can I say? Desperate times call for desperate effing measures.

And besides, Mike had forgiven me, too.

• • •

We all poured out of a cab in front of Mike's estate. "Home" does not describe it well enough. Honestly, it looked like a mini White House. The house was all white, prestigious pillars at the forefront, the black gate keeping all commoners out (in theory)—a house of means. The Corneliuses were my Barack and Michelle, and I was about to go ask the First Son if he could help me go on a witch hunt. In my defense, he'd volunteered. And he'd invited us here, which did not speak well for his judgment.

As I stood on the sidewalk out front and pondered—while we all waited for Karl to remember where he was—I felt like I was in a really, really bad knockoff of *Pretty Little Liars*. Instead of four hot teens looking to solve a murder, we were four disgraced people looking for absolution. I also felt that pit in my stomach, the one I had felt when I heard Mike leave me that voicemail.

Press on. Press on.

My legs somehow carried me up to the door, and I knocked.

Mike opened up and stood there in all his Black Ken Doll glory. He was in his sweats, meaning he'd been at the computer. He smiled. Behind his smile, there was something else. Sadness, guilt, pity? Maybe a mixture of all three. I went in for a hug, and he hugged me back. He hugged me back so hard that I didn't feel bad for making the move.

Do you know that feeling you get when you feel like someone may never look at you the same way again? Like they may never look at you like they knew you better than almost anyone? And the feeling you get when you see that it's still there? That the knowing is still in their eyes? Yes, it was that.

Alex cleared her throat. "As fun as this is, I'd love to hear why we're here and get the hell off the porch with this smelly slob."

I felt embarrassed to be having this moment with Mike in front of this ragtag group, and then I quickly stopped caring. I realized that I needed to be okay with being more vulnerable. Why not start on the porch of the Cornelius residence? I know: big adult thoughts on my part.

Mike pulled us inside and brought us into the living room. I remembered the last time I was there, before my fall. Having dinner, trying not to break all the collectibles with my eyes. He sat down on the couch. On the coffee table in front of him was a lime-green-and-blue laptop. It had rounded edges that appeared to be made out of rubber. It looked like a toy, almost—for a toddler.

I sat on the other couch directly across from him, and as he opened it, I saw the illuminated words: "SKOOLS 4 ALL."
Shit.

CHAPTER SIXTEEN

Karl (March 30, 2014)

I was starting to grow accustomed to Egyptian linens. Again I'd gone from dead sleep to splitting headache in a terrible instant. At least I was still ensconced in luxurious bedding. My first thought was that I was back in the company condo, that maybe my disastrous television debut was just a dream. Maybe *today* would be my big day to flail and fail for all to see.

I looked up, honestly half-expecting to see the smiling Skool twins on the monitor above the bed. In its place was a large oil painting of a serene landscape in an understated gold frame.

My eyes traversed the bedroom and its finery. This place was more tasteful than the new-money interior where I'd been waking up for the past two weeks (without ever remembering going to bed). Well, at least one thing remained consistent: I had no idea how I'd gotten here, my last memory being of a shrimp boat captain dissolving my black Amex card in a beaker of acid. Or was that a dream, too?

Okay. Remain calm. Where am I? Where the f—?

My heart began to race. It wasn't just the after-effects of the bender. I was legitimately panicked. Where had the night gone? Maybe I had somehow parlayed my dismal fall from false grace into a drunken seduction and/or pity lay? Maybe I'd bedded a sympathetic rich girl. I'd settle for a cougar, though at my age the youngest eligible cougars tend to be in their sixties . . .

But the more I looked around, the more I felt a guest-room vibe.

I caught a whiff of expensive coffee. I saw my boots and the rest of my black wardrobe plopped by the side of the bed. This, too, suggested a reluctant yet dutiful removal rather than fitful undressing during a burst of passion. Plus I was still wearing my socks and boxers.

After sliding out of bed, I pulled on my expensive failure pants, then donned my overpriced loser shirt. Put my trendy bum boots on, too, in case I needed to make a run for it. I looked out the mahogany-framed window. I could see a peaceful tree-lined block of brownstones—but far away, beyond a wide lawn and black gate. It could be Brooklyn Heights, Fort Greene, or some other respectable neighborhood where I'd never afford to own.

I opened the door and padded softly into the hallway. A stately grandfather clock stood at the other end. I walked along a richly woven Persian runner, flanked by a dark wood banister and a wall of framed family photos.

Aha! I thought, feeling like an amateur detective. Here were clues.

The series began with a grainy black-and-white print of a proud young black couple standing in front of a simple wooden shack. It looked like it might have been taken during the Civil War. From there, the images progressed through the generations, its subjects growing older and more prosperous, their family expanding and giving way to new generations of attractive black folks who in turn appeared to progress and prosper more than the previous generations. Wedding photos begat baby pictures, which led to graduations, then more wedding photos, and on and on.

I didn't recognize anyone in the photos until I got to the framed color print at the end of the hall. It featured a middle-aged couple and their teenage son smiling on a sailboat with the Obamas. Yes, *those* Obamas: Barack*, Michelle, Sasha, and Malia. I recognized the Obamas, but not the other family. Although their teenage son looked vaguely familiar . . .

The smell of coffee grew stronger, pulling me downstairs.

When I hit the first-floor landing, I followed the sound of muffled voices into the formal dining room. Piano concerto music played softly in the background. There in the flesh was that attractive couple from the sailboat. They were looking over the shoulder of their handsome son as he sat at the middle of the table aggressively typing away on what looked like a toy laptop. Where one might expect to see a glowing Apple logo were the words "SKOOLS 4 ALL"—emblazoned in green letters against a bright blue background.

Sitting on either side of the big kid at the little kid computer were Alex and Coretta. I swallowed. I suddenly wished I'd checked myself in the mirror.

A nerdy white girl, about Coretta's age, leaned against the back of Coretta's chair. She looked vaguely familiar, as well...

With expressions ranging from confusion to awe, everyone in the room appeared transfixed by the kiddie computer's screen, hidden from my view.

"Good morning?" I offered tentatively.

Nerdy white girl registered a distinct ISS look; Coretta looked up and smiled tentatively; Alex accompanied the weary rolling of her eyes with a judgmental shaking of her head; the kid on the computer was too engrossed in what he was doing to look up; the same was true for his father.

The only person who greeted me like a fellow human being was the nice lady from the sailboat photo. She clutched a steaming mug of coffee that I desperately coveted.

"Well, good morning! You must be Karl," she said cheerfully. She made her way around the table to greet me with a friendly handshake. "I'm Esther Cornelius. Welcome to our home. How did you sleep?"

"Like a man disgraced," I answered in my most boastful Errol Flynn voice.

"That's the spirit!" Mr. Cornelius boomed.

I tried my best to smile. He was only a few years older than I was, but he was decades beyond me in experience, depth, and worldliness—not to mention wealth, power, and the weight of his wristwatch. He regarded me with a friendly smile. "How 'bout some coffee, Karl? How do you take it? Regular?"

"I'll get the coffee, dear," Mrs. Cornelius insisted. "You all keep at it in here. Karl, how would you like your coffee?"

"Cream, two sugars, please. Thank you."

"I respect a young man with good manners," Mr. Cornelius added. "Now please forgive my bad ones. I'm Douglas Cornelius, and this is my son Mike. Karl, please come around to this side of the table so I can shake your hand and show you what we've got so far."

"Great. Um, can't wait to see . . . what you've . . . got?" I paused before walking over. Alex, Coretta, and the other girl eyed me intently. "I'm sorry; did I meet you last night? My memory has been compromised lately. Coretta, you must be Coretta. I mean, I know you are Coretta. I mean, I know you. You know . . . This is weird. I'm sorry. It's just . . . This is weird."

Coretta smiled at my squirming. "What's weird, Karl? Not remembering meeting me last night? Or being face-to-face with someone whom you've already literally attempted to embody? Or suffering the exact same disgrace that I suffered two weeks ago, then getting plastered and waking up in my boyfriend's parents' house?" She laughed.

At the word "boyfriend," the kid at the computer looked up for the first time. He was the same kid from the photos. It all made sense . . . at least the location part. I knew *where* I was, at least. I just didn't know why or how or what the hell it meant. I made my way around the table to join the gang.

Coretta pushed her chair back from the table and stood up to greet me. "I'm just messing with you, Karl."

She stepped forward. It appeared she was attempting to give me an awkward hug. Yes, this was happening.

A hug.

I was equally awkward in my attempt to reciprocate it. But when a hug comes, that's what you do. I supposed I should be thankful. She could have punched me in the face. That would have been more appropriate, and certainly less unexpected. We ended up sort of patting the outsides of each other's shoulders, then stepping back and looking each other curiously in the eyes.

Weirder than the hug was finally meeting Coretta face-to-face after months of trying to write like her—capped off with the unsettling estrangement that ended our work arrangement.

On the other hand, I had a queasy inkling we'd met before. For better or worse, I was growing accustomed to a blank memory on any given morning in regard to the people and events of the previous night.

Mike stood up to formally shake my hand. "I'm Mike

Cornelius, Coretta's boyfriend." He flashed a glance at Coretta as if for reassurance that it was okay to echo her word choice.

"Yep, that's my boyfriend," Coretta chirped. "But until this morning I had no concept of his true computer genius."

"Well, he had us all fooled." Douglas Cornelius gave his son's shoulders a playful squeeze. "Didn't you, son?"

"Yeah, I guess so." Mike shrugged modestly before taking his seat and returning his attention to the kiddie laptop.

Esther entered the room, handed me a giant mug of coffee, and winked. "When we came home last night, we figured he was playing video games. Or looking at porn."

"Mom!" Mike groaned.

His mother shot me a grin. "But it turns out we've had a real-life computer hacker living under our roof this entire time."

"And lucky for us," Douglas added gravely, his smile fading. He turned to his wife. "We were so stupid. To think, Esther, that we both hold positions on the board of directors of their SKOOLS 4 ALL foundation—"

"Dad, you guys are not stupid!" Mike protested. "These people had a lot of folks fooled. Including me!"

"Including my parents," Nerd Girl interjected. "They hold a seat on the board, too."

I assumed that Nerd Girl was Coretta's best friend (Rebecca? Ruthie?), the one she always talked about letting down, but I wanted to make sure. I also wondered if introducing myself might make her ease up on the hostile eye-daggers she kept aiming my way. "Hi, I'm Karl, by the way." I extended a hand. "You must be Coretta's friend . . ."

"Rachel." She shook my hand mechanically. Her lip was still curled in a frown, her nose slightly wrinkled. (Like I said, pure ISS.) "We actually met last night. But I guess you don't remember. You were pretty wasted."

"Yeah, I guess I was. Sorry about that. Rough night."

"You might also know me as 'Noprah,'" she added with a smirk.

I shot Alex a look, which she answered with a smirk of her own. It told me, *not now*. Best to address the group. "Um, well, I figured the Skools were up to no good. But they're really criminals?"

Douglas Cornelius took a deep breath and blew it out emphatically, as if there were a lit birthday cake in front of his face. "You have no idea. So far it looks like bank and securities fraud, bribery and extortion, illegal government contracts, Privacy Act violations . . . the list goes on."

"And those are just crimes that are on the books," Esther added. "Some of the things they've been doing with their so-called 'charter school' program are even more insidious. It's difficult to imagine a motive."

"Well, money might have something to do with it," Alex deadpanned.

"They stand to make a fortune from state school vouchers alone," Mike confirmed. "Especially once their cyber-schools become licensed and approved. But you want to know what led me down this crazy rabbit hole to start with? It was you guys. I mean, the blog. The viral sensation that was *Little White Lies*."

I squinted at this nice young man and shook my head in confusion.

"I hacked their emails. Which was ridiculously easy. It's their Achilles heel. But it turns out they were setting up false accounts to boost the followers of *Little White Lies* from the beginning. They *helped* it go viral. And it was all to

get the audience for the show they really wanted all along:
Takin' U to Skool."

After my second cup of coffee, I was no longer confused. Well,
I *was*. But I was mostly angry. And hungry. Still, mostly angry.
   Not so much about how the Skools had manipulated
Coretta's social media status. I would have loved her Tumblr
if she'd had seventy followers. So would everyone else; it
would have gone viral eventually. They'd wasted their time
with that. No, it was that these sociopathic clowns believed
that *they* had the charisma to host a TV show for teens.
   Of course, that wasn't their original plan. They'd
intended for Coretta to host for a while. They'd hoped to
brainwash her. But the emails Mike had hacked also made
plain that Coretta's confession—about her, about me, about
AllYou™—provided the perfect excuse to fast-track *Takin'
U to Skool* . . . whatever the hell *that* show was going to be.
   "You're disgusted with the Skools, aren't you, Karl?"
Esther Cornelius said, reading my ISS expression. "I share
your disgust at how they plan to subvert our very educational
system with school vouchers. It offends me, too."
   Oh. Right. That.
   I nodded.
   "Let me fill you in on some of the particulars, Karl."
Douglas glanced down at Mike. "Do you mind, son? Or
would you rather tell him?"
   "Go ahead, Dad." Mike barely paused from his furious
keystroking on the little laptop. "I need to concentrate on this
right now. I think I'm onto something here."
   I noticed Coretta staring at Mike with gooey eyes. I tried
to remember my own adolescence, if I'd ever looked at a girl
that way. Nope. I'd never even looked at Alex that way.

"The Skools have been developing a cyber-school program," Douglas explained. "Your cyber-bullying post was prescient, Karl. They're very close to being certified as an alternative, quote-unquote 'charter school' in a number of states. As such, the Skools will be eligible to receive state-issued education vouchers to the tune of thousands of dollars per child for providing an alternative to public education. And to drive their enrollment up, they're offering kickbacks of up to fifty percent of the voucher value to the parents—or administrators—who enroll their kids in the school."

"Administrators?" He'd fully captured my interest. The plan sounded diabolical.

"They're targeting incarcerated youth." Esther looked at me, her expression dark. "As well as children in foster homes."

I began to feel queasier.

"That way they can rack up multiple vouchers at one time," Coretta added.

"Oh, wow." In spite of their lax email security, the Skools were starting to seem smarter and more purely evil than I'd ever imagined.

"And check out these crazy lesson plans they're teaching in their crazy cyber school!" Rachel blurted out. "Mike, show him. It's completely insane! They've got this entire unit for world history on Leopold the Second, 'Builder King.' Do you know who Leopold the Second is?"

"Yeah, he's that crazy Belgian king who started the Free Congo State so he could chop everyone's hands off," I heard myself say.

Not bad, Karl, I thought. Even Douglas and Esther seemed impressed. I didn't admit that I'd learned of Leopold II of Belgium from the teachings of Star (of Star and Buc Wild*) aka

Troi Torain, the infamous hip-hop shock jock who coined the philosophy Objective Hate. That wasn't my Harvard education talking.

"Exactly!" Rachel seemed happy to make an intellectual connection with me, and I was glad to oblige. "He took his own private army into Africa and enslaved, mutilated, and murdered an entire indigenous population. And these sick weirdos are presenting him to children as some great man who beautified Belgium. A shining example of European beneficence."

"Why would they be teaching that?!" I demanded. "What are they, his grandkids or something?"

"Did you say Free Congo State?" Mike looked up from his key-tapping with what seemed like a delayed reaction. "One of the Skools' subsidiaries in Africa is called Free Congo . . ."

In spite of my hangover—or maybe because of it—a thought occurred to me. I texted Kris and Sarah:

> PLEASE FIND OUT IF SKOOLS
> ARE DESCENDENTS OF KING
> LEOPOLD II OF BELGIUM

"Babe, remember that cyber-bullying post you wrote?" Mike said. "Kinda hard-core. You were pretty freaked out about it when it stirred up so much controversy. I remember you saying that you weren't yourself when you wrote it."

"She was actually me when she wrote that one," I said.

"Right, Karl. I got that." Mike's voice was flat, but I noticed his father shoot him a stern side-eye, which softened his delivery. "Anyway, there was that thing at the end about SKOOLS 4 ALL. I thought there was something really weird about distributing satellite-connected laptops to children in rural Africa. So I started looking into—" Mike paused and looked down at the laptop. "Hold on a sec. This script is almost finished."

Oh, yeah, now I remembered the bit about SKOOLS 4 ALL. But I still didn't remember being put to bed in the Cornelius guest room . . .

"Oh, *shit!*"

It was the loudest exclamation of the morning—from mild-mannered Mike.

"What is it, son?" Douglas and Esther harmonized.

I looked down at the screen to see if I could see what Mike saw. But all I could discern was a jumble of zeroes and ones.

"Just what I thought: the research tools on these laptops direct students *only* to the educational content portals designed and/or approved by the Skools."

"To lessons like that 'Builder King' bullshit," I felt compelled to throw in.

"Right," Mike acknowledged. "But you'll recall that I also determined that their proprietary Internet browsers are gated in a far more permissive configuration, so that these laptops also function as a massive data collection network."

Rachel nodded. "So when the kids aren't doing 'Skoolwork,' they get to surf the web at will. And the Skools can sell their individual and aggregate data to whoever has the euros."

"Right," Mike remained even-keeled in spite of his exhilaration. "I knew about the Skools' data collection conglomerate, but I didn't realize that SKOOLS 4 ALL was part of it. And I never really questioned why all these laptops had such souped-up satellite Wi-Fi capabilities. The encryption was totally post-futurist, but I knew I could get through."

I glanced at Coretta, who appeared to regard Mike as if he were some kind of intergalactic god. Rachel had a similar look, though without any presumption that she would be allowed to touch him.

F$$P vibrated in my hand. I checked the new text from Kris:

> YES. A & K R GRANDCHILDREN OF LUCIEN PHILIPPE MARIE ANTOINE (1906–1984), DUKE OF TERVUREN— ILLEGITIMATE SON OF LEO 2

"Eureka!" I yelled. "The Skool twins are the grandchildren of Leopold II's illegitimate son!"

Nobody seemed particularly interested in this revelation.

It made sense at the moment; in the grand scheme of evil revelations, this was fairly minor. (But at least my flunkies were finally getting around to their opposition research.) No, everyone was much more interested in Mike, who clapped his hands together. "The reason these laptops need such burly networking capabilities is because each one of these machines is a tiny cog in a huge, massive, global money-laundering scheme—and it's all run by the Skools and their family members in Belgium and Africa."

Mrs. Cornelius gasped. "That's horrible!"

"It is horrible, Mom," Mike answered matter-of-factly. "Dark pools."

"What do you know about dark pools?" Mr. Cornelius whispered.

"What are dark pools?" Coretta asked Mike dreamily. "And who *are* you?"

Mike smiled at Coretta but regained his game face.

"Alternative economies we aren't supposed to know about. Kind of like Bitcoins, before everyone knew about them. Do you know what Bitcoins are, Rachel?"

Rachel looked down at the floor. "I think so. How do they work again?"

Mike struggled to remain patient. "You know how BitTorrent works?"

Rachel blushed. "Yes, I know how BitTorrent works."

"Bitcoins are like BitTorrent for money. Transactions are divided among thousands of individual computers, each one processing a fraction of the transaction. So that the movement of money is virtually untraceable. Or so people think."

Rachel processed out loud for the whole group. "So the Skools are going to use all these little blue laptops to break up their money into tiny little bits, and then move it around and hide it in secret banks?"

"Pretty much," Mike answered with a satisfied grin.

"And we can prove this?" Douglas asked.

"Pretty much," Mike repeated, turning back to the laptop. "I just need a few more hours."

"My God." Mr. Cornelius yanked his son out of his seat and pulled him into a hug. "You done good, son. You done good."

CHAPTER SEVENTEEN

Coretta (April 4, 2014)

Karl and I sat in a dressing room together at Pulse TV.

I say "a" dressing room, but really it was *my* dressing room a month ago. I had only used it once, and I didn't have any dressing to do in it, but it felt strange to be back. Perhaps because this time, every security guard in the building was watching our every move. And yes, I mean *every* move. Luckily I didn't have to use the bathroom. I'd seen hidden camera shows, and I wasn't going to be a statistic! (At least not that kind of statistic.)

You see, dear reader, Karl and I had asked the Skools if we could make a public apology. We'd told them that we wanted to do it together and that we thought it would be best to do it before the debut of their new TV show, the one that was taking the *Little White Lies* time slot.

Seeing as the Skools were going to be hosting a teen talk show of their own, they thought that our mea culpa and blessing—"the blessing of the fallen," as Karin put it—could be beneficial.

A couple of days earlier, Rachel and I met once again in my bedroom.

Then, as before, I didn't feel like I had the strength to look her in the eye just yet. She was my best friend. I knew she was there for me, but I still felt so much shame—for where I was at in my life and where our friendship was at. It didn't help that she felt ashamed, too; it only made things worse.

I looked at the walls of my room and remembered when this was only a den of teenage dreams for us both. What our next thrift store outing would bring, what boy we would text and laugh about, what juicy school gossip we would share. Nothing of any weight, just laughs about the present.

But that was gone, and shit got real. I'd made this bed, so I might as well lie in it and recognize it for what it was. I told Rachel that I needed to make a public apology with Karl. Not to use a church term, but I needed to cleanse myself. He felt the same. It was a tall order—especially given how Mike could have gone public at any time with what we now knew about the Skool twins—not to mention that it was hard to predict the end result. But I guess that's life.

"Are you sure that this is what you want to do, Coretta? That this is what is best?"

I could tell by the way Rachel had asked that she knew that it was the best thing to do. Even as much as it might hurt, and as scary as it was to think about. "Yeah, Rach, I'm sure. If you're with me, I can do it. Please tell me you'll go with me."

"If we can get the twins of the Illuminati to give me clearance, I'm there a thousand times over."

Of course she was.

We would have exactly two minutes to read our agreed-upon mea culpa.

Karl and I had written it together, and the Skools had

approved it. We used fewer jokes and way fewer Beyoncé references than in our previous collaborations. We'd agreed to be escorted out of the building after our last word. Forever.

As I sat next to Karl on the stiff white IKEA couch, I looked straight ahead into the dressing room mirror. I locked eyes with his reflection.

A melancholy haze lingered over both of our faces.

Okay, I was feeling dramatic. It *was* dramatic. I silently compared our moment to rebellious soldiers in hiding together just before battle: we were armed with spears, facing an enemy armed with guns. Granted, I'd been studying such warfare a lot in the wake of learning about King Leopold II and his battle for the Belgian Congo.

I'm not sure what Karl was thinking, but I was for sure wondering (as I had a thousand times) how I'd gotten myself into this. How I found myself sitting next to Karl Ristoff, backstage in a TV studio, sweating so hard that my armpits smelled like onions and chicken noodle soup.

Our preapproved mea culpa, or "agreement to fault," began with a painful apology from me. It ended with a short but equally painful apology from Karl.

Then he was supposed to hand over the stage to the Skool Twins and their new show, *Takin' U to Skool.*

Then we were both supposed to disappear forever.

My parents thought it best to have a caucus at the Cornelius home to discuss what exactly was going to take place on air—before, well, it happened *on air.* They've always let me make my own decisions, and be my own person, but I've since learned that they actually do possess the wisdom that comes with being thirty or so years older than I am.

The gang was back together, minus Karl and Alex.

My parents, the Corneliuses, Mike, and Rachel gathered in the entirely too-formal living room. All strategies were welcome. My dad began.

"Now, Coretta, you can't just go up there and think that being cute and whatever is going to make people listen to you."

"Thanks for that, Dad."

"I'm just saying that you're going to have this Karl Ristoff guy next to you, who, and I'm just going to say it, looks like a questionable character. We have to acknowledge that this is a weird optic. A beautiful African-American teen girl side by side with a white man who looks like he builds computers and owns stock in Nabisco. How do we know that he isn't going to throw you under the bus once the lights come up? What do we even know about this guy?"

"Now let's not get into what Karl looks like," my mother, the great equalizer, chimed in. "I've spoken with Alex Melrose. I believe he's on the level. Let's just try to keep everyone on the same page and have a game plan."

I told my dad what he needed to know. That Karl, as sour and road-haggard as he looked, did have a good heart. That he'd honestly got as caught up in all of this nonsense as I had. And he *was* quite skilled at what he did and had a reputation to reclaim, far more than I did. If we told Karl what the plan was, he would be on board, one hundred percent.

One minute till air. Karl and I both took a deep breath.

For some reason, I shook hands with him. He broke into a wide smile, and I nervously smiled back. We rose in unison, looked at the dressing room door, then back at each other. Our double-locked gaze said it all. We knew what we had agreed to do, and we also knew what we *had* to do.

As soon as we exited and approached the set, those

ridiculous lights started flashing. Then it went black. The lights came up again, and the camera pointed at Karin and Anders as they both stood center stage. God, they looked ridiculous and perfect at the same time. But they were dressed . . . differently. They appeared hipper, younger, more approachable. More attractive. Anders had on gray jeans, wingtip shoes, and a plaid shirt. No tie, no jacket. Karin wore a white minidress that for once did not make her look like the Evil White Witch of the Woods. A wolf in sheep's clothing?

The cameraman began the countdown: "Five . . . four . . . three . . ." Then he stopped talking.

"Hello, America!" Karin announced in a bright voice. "Hello, world. I am Karin Skool, this is my brother Anders Skool, and this is . . . *Takin' U to Skool*, the teen talk show that will give an *honest* voice to your generation. But before we dig into the topics for tonight, we have two brief guests who'd like to say something to you all."

Anders came offstage and led us both by the arm into the spotlight. I tried not to squint under the brightness and heat. My heart was thumping even harder than when I'd first come to this place.

"Hello!" Anders said. "Now before you guys go and boo them off the stage, haha, please hear what they have to say. Karin and I want to make abundantly clear that *everyone* deserves a forum to express regret. Yes, even in the face of such loathsome behavior. That is the spirit in which we offer our new show. Thusly, we have agreed to let them speak to you tonight.

"Coretta, Karl, the floor is yours."

In that instant, my mind flashed back to Mike's kitchen, where he and I had gone to be alone after hatching the plan.

We'd left Rachel and Mike's parents alone with Karl and Alex Melrose. I remember giggling at the thought of those five people—so weird and different, really with no business hanging out at all, yet totally united and connected—discussing logistics.

"Coretta, are you okay?" Mike asked.

I stopped giggling. "I'm okay. I feel pretty great, actually."

He took my hands. "I know you're worried, and I would be worried, too. It's natural. But I need you to remember that I know what I'm doing, and I'm not going to let you down. You and Karl show up to do your part, and I'll show up to do mine. We have an inside man now, too, remember? It'll work out."

I nodded. I did remember, of course. Our inside man was none other than little Ethan. He had been the subject of quite a few scathing emails from his employers—they'd called him a "spineless yes-man"; a "PR embarrassment"; and most memorably "minion shit-show"—which Mike had gleefully hacked and then shared with him. After that, Ethan became quite eager to join our cause.

"It wasn't as if they would promote me," he'd told Mike.

I looked at Mike's sweet, sweet face. I hoped he was right about it working out. But even if he wasn't, we were still doing the right thing.

Now, scrolling on the screen behind us, was our apology for all to see.

I looked into the teleprompter, and we were off to the races.

"For those of you who don't know who we are, I am Coretta White, creator of the blog *Little White Lies*, which, as most of you know, was set to become a television show on Pulse TV. The man standing next to me is Karl Ristoff, who worked briefly as a ghostwriter for my blog. You might remember both of us from separate yet equally unfortunate Pulse TV debuts.

"We are here to say that we are sorry for the parts that we played in his whole ordeal. We are sorry to our family, our friends, our peers, teachers, mentors, and especially you, our viewers and readers and the public at large. I didn't consider myself a dishonest person, so when I found myself in this mess, my conscience mandated this apology so I could take a real breath again.

"I, Coretta White, employed Karl Ristoff to write some of the content for *Little White Lies*, and I was passing it off as my own. For this, I am very ashamed and sorry."

I nodded to Karl. He took a deep breath. Okay, he was over-acting a little with his ponderous expression, but it was too late now. "I have no defense in any of this," he said, "and I don't wish to rehash it all. I only want to say that I'm sorry, and also to say that both Coretta and I would like to wish Anders and Karin the best of luck with their new show *Takin' U to Skool*. Thank you."

That was our cue. Peering through the lights, I spotted Rachel behind the teleprompter with her headphones in her ears. She gave me the nod to let me know it was all going as planned. And with that, the words on the teleprompter shifted.

"Before Karl and I leave, we wanted to thank the Skools for having us here tonight," I piped up, taking a step forward and staring right into the camera. "We did a lot of soul-searching, and frankly, truth-searching, which led us down a path that we wanted to share with you . . ."

I was aware of movement and murmuring at the side of

the stage. Karin and Anders knew something was wrong—immediately. I couldn't waste any time; this was the critical window where they could pull the plug. I steeled myself and plowed forward, per our rehearsals:

"Seeing how Karl and I are being held accountable to ourselves, our families, and the public at large, mostly with the help of Karin and Anders, we thought: *What better way to repay them than to return the favor?* Karin, Anders, please come join us."

They stopped fidgeting. It worked. Now they were beyond the point of no return. They couldn't shut down the broadcast, because the audience was hooked. They were both hate-smiling from the wing. Hate-smiling: You know when you smile, but really you're clenching your jaw and hating each and every word that you are hearing and everything you are seeing? Yes, that. The audience started cheering, and Karl and I joined them.

Karl walked over to Karin and Anders and led them back onstage, much as Anders had led us to the stage moments ago. "Coretta and I wanted to thank you for sending us on this mission for truth," Karl said.

A scrolling PowerPoint presentation appeared on the screen behind us with the snappy title *takin' the skools to school.* Karl pulled the small remote control from his pocket and cleared his throat. "Being that this is *Takin' U to Skool,* how about a history lesson?

"First, allow me to introduce myself. I'm Karl Ristoff. I graduated from Harvard University; I have clandestinely worked for the US State Department, the United Nations, and the US Council on Foreign Relations. I've coauthored several books on the *New York Times* Nonfiction Best Seller List, and yes, I have also worked as a ghostwriter and social media consultant for numerous luminaries whom I would prefer not to name. Suffice it to say you've heard of most of them. Now please allow me to introduce you all to a very important historical figure with whom you may not be as familiar—but who happens to be the great-grandfather of our esteemed hosts."

I shot a glance at Anders and Karin. They were still hate-smiling, still utterly poised, no doubt plotting how they would spin this once they figured out how to get us offstage without looking like they had something to hide.

Karl pressed the remote, and the text gave way to a black-and-white photo of a stern-looking white man with a huge hipster beard and a flouncy military uniform above the caption:

LEOPOLD II: BUILDER KING.

"If you were to enroll at one of the Skools' hundreds of charter 'schools'—which on their best days are propaganda tools masquerading as cyber-schools—then you would learn all about the magnificent deeds of this great monarch, Leopold II, the so-called 'Builder King' responsible for so many grand buildings and public works in Belgium."

Karin and Anders turned to each other. *Hurry up, Karl,* I silently urged.

Karl gestured with the remote, and a red slash appeared across the word BUILDER with the word BUTCHER painted in red above it.

The black-and-white photo was now digitally defaced with the same red splattered over the man's face and body. The remote control clicked, and the image of bloody Leopold gave way to a montage of black-and-white photos picturing Africans of various ages—each of them missing a hand.

"In fact," Karl continued more quickly, "Leopold the second was one of the most brutal and devastating imperialists in the history of mankind. He robbed the Congo region in Africa of its natural resources while systematically enslaving, mutilating, and murdering millions and millions of innocent people. And now two of his descendants have decided to pick up where he left off."

Now Anders was whispering in Karin's ear and peering at the studio crew. I held my breath.

Another click of the remote refreshed the screen behind us to reveal the following equation in boldface type:

SKOOLS 4 ALL = $$ 4 SKOOLS.

"Karin and Anders Skool, the grandchildren of Leopold's son Lucien Philippe Marie Antoine, wish to follow in their great-granddaddy's footsteps. Make no mistake, they intend to exploit children and their families—not just in Africa and in the United States of America, but throughout the entire world. And perhaps the most perverse part of their plot is that these twisted siblings have been enriching themselves at the expense of the disenfranchised, all under the guise of education and a progressive social agenda."

I think I must have had what is known as a "disassociative moment." Because instead of listening to Karl's presentation, I was once again flashing back to our arrival at the Pulse TV studios this morning, my parents on either side of me.

This is it.

We all looked at one another, took a deep breath, and

walked in. We saw the security guard, the one we'd arranged
for. We knew because he had a red ribbon pinned to his chest.

"If you're all headed to the studio, it's the elevator on the
left. If not, I'd say it'd be on the right, but then again, who
knows." The guard nodded, smiled, and handed my parents
access cards.

As we parted ways, I felt my phone buzz in my jacket. It
was a text from Mike.

> Ethan got me in. All set.

Then I was back. The audience was murmuring uncom-
fortably. Anders whispered furiously in Karin's ear, and she
nodded. Only then did they finally stop smiling.

Anders whirled around and shouted to the tech booth,
"Enough already! Cut the feed to the stage. These liars have
gone too far, okay? We all know they're lying . . ." But his
voice was lost in the swelling protest from the audience.

Karl stopped reading and grinned at me. He nodded
toward Karin, who for a brief second attempted to cover
up the words and images with her hands. And that was it,
the money shot. That one shining moment showed her as
desperate and demented—*in public*. It was all we needed to
legitimize Karl's revelations; nothing could possibly be more
damning. And she knew it. She shook her head, glaring at
Anders for some sort of solution.

He shrugged and bolted for the side of the stage. She had
no choice but to clatter after her twin on her very high heels.

I don't remember much after that, except for giggling. I mean,
it *was* funny. But yes, I still giggle at inappropriate times.

Waiting in the wings were the same security guards who

had been watching our every move. Next to them my parents, the Corneliuses, Rachel, and Ethan. Yes, tiny little Ethan, the Skools' protégé. The one who'd allowed Mike access early this morning. He had actually been instrumental in giving us access to quite a bit of privileged information—and more importantly, in getting Mike into the tech booth, so we could stage the coup.

The Skools' escape route was blocked by an army.

Esther Cornelius stepped forward. "Karin, Anders, it stops here. You've been found out; the whistle has been blown. You're done."

The twins stood there in silence. They glanced at each other. They had no rebuttal. I think everyone expected some sort of fight. Instead, Anders muttered something about their lawyers. As in, the twins needed to see them.

Then the Skools raised their chins and joined hands. (So creepy.)

After that, they were perfectly calm. (Creepier.)

They allowed themselves to be escorted out of the building by the security officers. Karl and I witnessed all this from the stage. The audience watched it on the screen behind us. Then I saw the red and blue flashing lights. *What the hell?*

As soon as the twins reached the sidewalk, they were greeted by a posse of law enforcement officers that included NYPD, state police, and federal agents as well as a swelling scrum of paparazzi.

The police!

Amazing. Perfect. The police were never a part of our plan. We'd anticipated that a public shaming outside the building would probably be involved, but not the actual law. It turned out the Corneliuses—with the help of the Bernsteins and my parents—got the actual attorney general involved. Which led to actual arrest warrants and actual cops.

The moral of the story? It's best not to piss off a group of lawyers.

I didn't have a speech planned for after it all went down. But when I turned and squinted at the camera, I saw the telltale red blinking light. It was still recording. I was still on TV, live. And now I felt something rising up inside me. I looked at Karl. He nodded at me and smiled encouragement. As I looked at Mike in the booth and the faces of the teens from all over New York City in the audience, the words . . . just came out.

"So as you can see, there's a lot more to this story than any of us thought possible. I don't know what the future holds for me or for Karl or for *Little White Lies*, or even for Pulse TV . . . but I do know that we will do everything we can to make sure it is all rooted in truth and social justice from now on. This world is a scary place, and if you're not careful, it's easy to be swept into its dark corners. I know I was. But this world can also be a beautiful place. It *is* a beautiful place."

Here I had to pause. Mostly out of surprise.

Karl was dabbing at his eyes.

Amazing. I'd moved the guy. I took a deep breath and finished.

"So maybe if we all do our best to seek truth and justice while working to expose injustice and deception, and if more and more of us do that on a daily basis, then perhaps we will need fewer and fewer little white lies to get ourselves through the days. I'm Coretta White, and this has been *Takin' U to Skool*. Thank you."

EPILOGUE

Karl (Summer 2014)

Yeah, so that stuff all happened.

Um, any questions?

Who? What? How? When? Where? Why?

Okay, let's start with *where*. I'm writing this final chapter from my new apartment. It's in Fort Greene, and I own it! Alex and I made up after the whole revenge/justice scenario went down (Operation *Skools Out*), and she told me about another super-secret bank account.

Unbeknownst to me, for the past twenty years, Alex had been siphoning off twenty percent of all my AllYou earnings, placing half the money in an IRA (stands for "individual retirement account"; not being condescending—I never knew what it meant, either). She placed the other half in an investment account that's now worth over a million bucks.

I'm not exactly set for life, but it was enough to buy a decent apartment in a nice part of Brooklyn and a tiny shack in the Catskills. I've been able to take some much-needed time off after deciding to embark on an indefinite leave of absence from all social media. And hopefully by the time I'm sixty, if the human race and/or the United States still exist, I might be able to retire for real.

Thank you, Alex.

In case you are wondering, Dear Reader, whether Alex and I got back together after this whole ordeal, the answer is a resounding *NO!* However, much to her elation, I did decide to retire from rapping. Good-bye, MC Expensive Meal. And after a lot of encouragement from my ex-girlfriend, former boss, and Friend For Life (FFL), I've finally started writing my first novel. No title yet, but it takes place in the 1990s and follows the international misadventures of an Ivy League–educated PowerPoint specialist who secretly works for the CIA* and— even more secretly—is the son of Huey P. Newton*.

I'm happy to report that I've also disabled my Tinder and OkCupid profiles. It's kind of a long story, and I'm going to spare you the details, but lately I've been spending a lot of time enjoying the company of Chloe Delvoye, the young woman I met on the Pulse TV "limo boose." I probably shouldn't even be mentioning it, but there it is. (Hi, Chloe.) And to her credit, she quit Pulse TV the morning after our bus ride, disgusted with the Skools.

A few more notes on *where* along with a bit of *how*:

The Skool twins also reside in Brooklyn, where they are still being detained at the Metropolitan Correctional Center, affectionately known as "Little Gitmo" because it is said to contain a number of high-level terror suspects. (I can't resist mentioning that Lil' Gitmo would be a pretty sweet name for a rapper. Just not me.) Between the connections that Coretta's and Rachel's fathers have with federal prosecutors and which the Corneliuses have in general—and thanks in large part to Mike's incredible hacker-sleuthing—the state department was able to quickly build a case against Anders and Karin.

The timing worked out perfectly. They served the arrest

warrant immediately after the twins' public humiliation on Pulse TV.

I also imagine that Coretta and I were able to serve such just desserts on live television because of some political power moves by Mr. White and Mr. Cornelius. Why would they allow us to do so? Four words spring to mind: Guilt, Justice, Revenge, Redemption.

As far as I know, the other principal characters from this saga—including my trusty cadre of subcontractors, Kris and Sarah, now otherwise employed—all remain in New York City, most of us in Brooklyn and none of us incarcerated.

Coretta graduated high school and will be enrolling at Harvard in the fall. I'm not sure if her decision to forego Stanford was due to her disdain for Condoleezza Rice* or because Mike is going to MIT, but I suspect the latter. I'm a little bit sorry to see two such amazing young people leaving Brooklyn for Boston (yuck!), but I suppose those are both good schools, and I'm sure neither one of them will decide to live there after they graduate. (Sorry, Boston.)

I can't remember where Rachel is going—probably her safety school. She and I have not stayed in touch, though not for her lack of trying.

Evidently Rachel is one of those people who's slow in warming up to others, but she doesn't hold tightly to first impressions. Since we'd gotten off on such hostile footing when we first met, Rachel Bernstein was the last member of our "Skools Out" squad I expected to hear from. But not only did she send me a handwritten card (as I imagine all of us got), Rachel also texted me several times with questions about recipes, shoe storage, shower curtain rings, Ohio, and other seemingly random subjects.

Typically her texts would come in bursts of five. Initially

I responded to all of them, but then I gradually reduced my number of replies to zero. Maybe it's society's pernicious influence, but there was something about being text buddies with a teenage girl that was starting to make me feel creepy. I mean, it's one thing if it's work related, but this kid is definitely *not* Oprah.

Alex is still ensconced in her Chelsea mega-loft, but even she is considering a move to Brooklyn as of late. (I'm not holding my breath.) Business is booming again at AllYou™. In typical Melrose fashion, Alex spun the negative impact from her association with the Skools into good fortune. She was able to warn a few of her clients who sat on the boards of SKOOLS 4 ALL and Pulse TV about the evil twins before the shit hit the fan.

So she not only scored some valuable brownie points, she also helped facilitate the secret board meetings that led to the ouster of the Skools from both Pulse TV and their SKOOLS 4 ALL foundation, which coincided with their dramatic arrest. There was some talk among the Corneliuses, the Whites, and the Bernsteins about installing a new board of directors that would take the foundation in a new direction.

Initially the Corneliuses even considered buying Pulse TV outright. But the intermingled finances between the network, the foundation, and the Skools' various other "nonprofits" and corporations are so cryptic, convoluted, and riddled with fraud that it will take months, if not years, to decipher (never mind assess) the largely illegal assets and accounts.

Also, dark pools.

Oh, and Mr. Cornelius has made a pledge to help find jobs for any SKOOLS 4 ALL or Pulse TV employees not implicated in illegal or unethical activity.

• • •

Are we still on *where*? Because speaking of pools, I'm happy to report that immediately after our triumphant trampling of those twisted siblings, Mr. and Mrs. Cornelius welcomed our entire crew—Alex and me, Coretta and her parents, Rachel (who for some reason brought her bubbi), and of course Mike—to fly on their private jet to their vacation home in Bermuda.

They call it a "vacation home," but it felt more like a private resort.

Ironically their spread is situated in between Bloomberg's and Oprah's. Yes, *real* Oprah. No, we didn't see her.

Let me say if you've never been to Bermuda and stayed at a billionaire's house, I highly suggest you do so.

The highlight of our stay came while Alex and I were sunbathing on their private beach, drinking tropical cocktails out of blown-glass coconuts. We looked up to see Coretta and Mike on the deck of his parents' sailboat, drinking what I have to assume was a nonalcoholic sparkling beverage.

We raised our glasses. The four of us, without missing a beat, reenacted the "Looking good, feeling good!" scene from *Trading Places**.

Unfortunately Coretta and Mike hadn't even heard of the movie (they still might not have), so they didn't get the reference, much less recognize the roles they were unwittingly playing. And that is very sad—for them.

So there was that.

Why did all of this happen? Well, we hope it was for a good reason. The Universe works in mysterious ways, and by the time you're reading this epilogue, there will no doubt be countless effects and side effects felt from the remarkable space in time that we have attempted to recount within these pages.

I could delve into the motives of the Skool siblings in targeting a seventeen-year-old girl and a hapless middle-aged man for destruction at the expense of their own odious empire. But since they are psychopathic freaks descended from evil incarnate, anything I write would be mere conjecture.

Having trolled through Mike's collection of hacked emails (thank you, Mike), it's clear why the Skools viewed Coretta as a perfect pawn/cloak for their insidious enterprises. It's because their own racism got in the way. They underestimated both her brilliance and moral backbone. They believed they could control her through their carefully cultivated relationship with the Corneliuses, and by the bounds of her restrictive Pulse TV contract.

But when Coretta sent them her heartfelt confession and they glimpsed her depth of character through her genuine struggle with this ethical dilemma, they must have realized that 1) they did not control her, and 2) they did not even know who she was. They had taken the words of her underpaid surrogate—a man old enough to be her father!—as the true gospel of Coretta and then found themselves duped. They feared Coretta's power, which they had helped to create, and were also butt-sore over her violation of their so-called trust.

So they engineered revenge.

As far as I'm concerned, they belong in Lil' Gitmo.

So what now?

The good news, of course: I'm not broke.

Coretta and Mike (and yes, Rachel) are going to college. And as much as my feelings are mixed about the University Industrial Complex, I recognize the value of a good education at a prestigious school. And seeing these bright youngsters on the road to continued success—as cheesy as that sounds, especially when read in the junior high vice-principal voice that's playing in my head right now—it honestly gives me hope for the future. And when I say "honestly" that is not to suggest that I am being in any way disingenuous.

I'm not sure if I'll keep in touch with Coretta, or if I'll even see her again.

It was weird enough working for a seventeen-year-old—now I'm going to be friends with her? Not that I have anything against young people; I just don't think I want to be that old dude hanging out at the college parties. But who knows? Maybe we'll get coffee together sometime. Maybe she and Mike will invite me to their wedding. If so, I hope it's in Bermuda! Or maybe this book will be a big hit, and Coretta and Karl will get their own TV show after all.

The bad news? You don't wanna hear the bad news. The bad news is that stop-and-frisk still exists. And so does Boko Haram. And now, apparently, something horrible called ISIS (not to be confused with Isis, the Egyptian goddess). The "War in Afghanistan" is soon coming to an "end." But not really. Meanwhile the "Iraq War" came to an "end" three years ago, and that country has never been more fucked up than it is now. Want to see something scary? Read the Iraq War page on Wikipedia. (I just did, and I'd like to throw up.)

But the bad news does bring to mind a conversation I had in Bermuda with my personal link to the top point-oh-one percent, Ms. Alex Rose, and my new favorite venture capitalists—Esther and Douglas Cornelius.

It took place a few hours after our *Trading Places* moment. I imagined Mike and Coretta were still happily sailing in the sunset. Coretta's parents were off taking a romantic walk on the beach, or so I also imagined. Rachel was swimming laps in the pool as her bubbi snoozed on a deck chair beneath a bright pink umbrella. Alex and I sat at one of the outdoor dining tables with Douglas and Esther—which was how they insisted we address them—enjoying fresh cocktails and snacking on tangy ceviche prepared by their housekeeper/driver/chef.

I sensed that our hosts were straining to make sense of two forty-somethings who for whatever reasons had never procreated.

Meanwhile, I struggled to imagine what it must be like to be raising a teenager. I figured it had to be some kind of nightmare—even if you are rich enough to have a house in Bermuda next to Oprah's. So I looked out across the turquoise water and said, "Man, life sucks, doesn't it?"

Esther let out a squeak of amusement.

Douglas played along. "Yeah, this is pretty horrible. Sorry to drag you guys out here."

Alex allowed herself to chuckle. "If I have to sit through one more of these crummy sunsets . . ."

"Ha. I know. And that gross water! Please don't make us go in there again." I slurped down a mouthful of ceviche, then self-consciously dabbed at my chin with my napkin. "Seriously, though, I can definitely see why Bloomberg spent every single weekend out here while he was mayor."

Esther leaned slightly toward Alex and me. "In case you were wondering, no, we did not name our son after Michael Bloomberg."

Oddly, I just had been wondering exactly that. I stopped myself from expressing relief at sparing their kid the specter of the Undisputed King of Stop-and-Frisk. Also, Alex was reading my mind; she hit me with a glare before I could open my mouth.

"It must be weird going back and forth between here and the city, especially with Mike—your Mike, I mean," I said. I was riding a nice rum-and-ceviche buzz and was thinking aloud. "Out here, it's like paradise. You know your kid is safe. I mean, aside from the Bermuda Triangle*. But otherwise you've got literally nothing to worry about."

"Except property taxes," Alex muttered.

Esther nodded thoughtfully. "We do worry. Of course our son is a very sensible young man, but we've also taught him the differences between the system and the individuals who are charged with enforcing the system. Between the government and those who represent it."

"Oh, yeah?" I smirked. "And what are those differences?"

Alex kicked my leg—hard—under the table.

Esther turned to her husband.

"Systems are flawed just like people are, Karl," Douglas offered. "Both are capable of change, but it never comes easy. Authority figures—whether they're teachers, police officers, or security guards, even parents—must be respected. Not that they can't be challenged. But they must be respected above all for the sake of peace and order. All too frequently for the sake of self-preservation. Even when they are wrong, even if they have not earned or do not deserve your respect."

I blinked. "Heavy."

Alex tilted her head just enough to silently criticize, *Heavy? That's the best you've got?*

"But those are heat-of-the-moment rules, at least to some degree," Douglas elaborated. "Respect for authority is a baseline expectation. And it should always be the default when interacting with people in their official capacities. That's true no matter what color or race you are."

"That's not to say you need to hold back," Esther clarified.

"It's crucial to express your opinions and beliefs when you're interacting with these same people in a social situation. Over a plate of food, over a drink, you can and should speak your mind—whether it's to your teacher, your preacher, or the mayor. As long as you conduct yourself in a respectful manner."

"And that's one way you can influence *individuals* to change," Douglas added. "Or at the very least, express your views and seek to broaden your outlook through friendly discourse. Of course, there are many ways to foment change within individuals . . . persuasive writing and debate, conscious artistic expression, progressive social media campaigns."

Wow, I thought. *Is this how billionaires talk over drinks?* I could practically see the ellipses floating through their air to punctuate his thesis.

"That's cool." I said. I ignored another kick under the table from Alex. "So how do you change the system? And please don't tell me by voting. Because I did vote—for Obama. Twice!"

"Well, Karl, I'm glad to hear that. We voted for him, too." Douglas chuckled and glanced at Esther. "We've also been fortunate to be able to converse with the Obamas over plates of food, much like we are doing right now."

I looked around, exaggerating my movements as if searching for the President and First Lady.

"Don't hold your breath, Karl," Douglas said with a smile.

"We do realize," Esther said, "that most people who struggle through this world never get to experience such a wonderful escape as this."

"They just stay stuck in the muck," Alex surmised bluntly.

• • •

In New York City, stop-and-frisk still goes on, even under our new mayor and, yes, the father of a boy with a large Afro, Bill de Blasio. Stop-and-frisk has other names and variations in other cities and towns—rollouts, investigatory stops, um . . . racial profiling—and the practice is thriving. Unarmed black men are being beaten and shot by the police with alarming frequency.

The United States is the world leader in incarceration, with more than two million citizens behind bars—a five-hundred-percent increase over the last forty years. The US now imprisons a larger percentage of its population than Russia or China. Black men are six times more likely to be incarcerated than white men, and Hispanic men are two and a half times more likely. For black men in their thirties, one in ten is in prison or jail on any given day.

Okay, enough bad news. I realize that I'm beginning to sound like a cranky old man. Hey, at least I can sleep at night knowing that incarcerated youth won't be targeted and mined by the Skools with bogus vouchers and plans for global reeducation. The rum helps, too.

Don't even get me started on Obama. I can't believe I used to like that guy! (Oh, well, he's gotta be better than McCain* or Romney*. And I guess if he's friends with the Corneliuses, then he can't be all bad.) And climate change? Fugeddaboudit! But seriously, *enough*. We all know that the world has gone to shit. And yes, cranky people over the age of thirty have probably been saying the same thing for the past five thousand years, at least. So what are we going to do about it?

The truth is, in all seriousness, I honestly don't know.

But I think what Coretta said in her impromptu speech at the end of the first and final episode of *Takin' U to Skool* is a good place to start: seek and empower truth and justice; recognize and oppose injustice and deception.

Beyond that, you tell me:

What are we going to do?

Beastie Boys (1981–2012) one of the greatest rap groups of all time.

Bermuda Triangle A weird zone in the Atlantic Ocean where, legend has it, countless ships and planes have disappeared—mysteriously and without a trace. The Bermuda Triangle was big in the '70s, even though most of the disappearances were said to have occurred decades before.

Birdman (1969–) You know who Lil Wayne is, but you don't know who Birdman is?? Not to be confused with the Academy Award–winning film *Birdman*, or the overly tattooed Caucasian NBA star also known as Birdman, this Birdman is the overly tattooed rapper—aka Baby—who cofounded Cash Money Records, and is reported to be worth well over a hundred million dollars. Lil Wayne—who once considered Baby his father figure (Birdman signed Lil Wayne when he was only twelve years old, and the two of them once released an album titled *Like Father Like Son*)—filed suit against Cash Money Records for some fifty-one million in monies due.

Johnny Cash (1932–2003) The Man in Black. Shot a man in Memphis just to watch him die. Or so the song goes. One of the heaviest dudes of the twentieth century. No irreverent Appendix entry will do Johnny Cash justice. Forget whatever preconceived ideas you may have about country music and seek out this man's recordings.

CIA The Central Intelligence Agency. An inaccurately named organization (also the wrong word). Probably best to leave it at that. I'm already on enough watch lists.

Pink Floyd (1965–1994; 2013–2014) was not a man but a band. I can't say I'm much of a fan. According to some folks, the band went downhill after the weird older dude, Syd Barrett, left in 1968. And then there's been a bunch of weird stuff between the two other main guys, I think. They did have some cool album covers. And "Another Brick in the Wall" was my favorite song when I was in eighth grade. I use the song "Money" as a ringtone on my R$$P because it's called "Money."

Errol Flynn (1909–1959) was an actor, adventurer, playboy, and scalawag who came and went before my time. I haven't seen his films, but he's been on my mind since I read his highly entertaining autobiography *My Wicked, Wicked Ways*. Swagger to the fullest. My treacly lilt does him no justice.

Killer Mike (1975–) Do you kids remember the rap group Outkast? Well, way back in 2004, Killer Mike was the Strong Man in that circus-themed video for "The Whole World," spitting that relentless verse while holding an old jalopy above his head. And now the future of non-bullshit rap music appears to be resting on his shoulders. You might know Killer

Mike as a spokesman for his community who has appeared on CNN and other news outlets, or as the heftier half of the two-man rap supergroup Run the Jewels, along with the great El Producto aka El-P.

Lil Wayne (1982–) Of course you know who Lil Wayne is.

John McCain (1936–) An old man who ran for president in 2008 and chose an Alaskan husky as his running mate. Back then Matt Taibbi wrote a profile about the old man called "Make-Believe Maverick" for *Rolling Stone* magazine. I highly recommend it.

The Meters (1965–1977; 1989–) are, after Louis Armstrong, arguably the greatest musical force to ever come from New Orleans. Armstrong played jazz. The Meters play funk.

Barney Miller A 1970s sitcom that took place in a fictional Greenwich Village NYPD precinct. Hal Linden plays the eponymous affable captain in charge of a staff of colorful detectives representing a range of ethnicities, but sorry, no women. And damn, they got a funky-ass theme song!

"Two Tickets to Paradise" A song by Eddie Money, the haggard and bloated rocker you see before you in 2013—in the double-breasted sport jacket, necklace over a turtleneck sweater, wheezing into the saxophone—was a beautiful young man who had it all in 1979. Born Edward Mahoney to a family of NYC cops, Eddie ditched the police academy, changed his last name to Money, and set out for California to pursue his dream: sex, drugs, and rock and roll. According to Wikipedia, rock impresario Bill Graham once said, "Eddie

Money has it all . . . Not only can he sing, write, and play, but he is a natural performer." The reason I use his cheeseball song as a ringtone on F$$P? The man's name is Money!

Huey P. Newton (1942–1989) Cofounder of the Black Panther Party.

Night Court A 1980s sitcom that took place in a Manhattan courtroom during the night shift. I've just learned from Wikipedia that the show's creator, Reinhold Weege, also worked on *Barney Miller*. The young, wacky judge is played by actor-magician Harry Anderson. Not much point in IMDB-ing that guy or, frankly, watching the show, but I do recommend checking out their theme song. Maybe not as funky as *Barney Miller*, but funky nonetheless. And the show's cast actually includes more than one female character.

Barack Obama (1961–) I'm not sure we need an entry in this Appendix for the forty-fourth President of the United States, Barack Hussein Obama. But now that I've written it, I can't stop staring at his amazing name. I suggest you try it. Right now. Stare at his name: Barack Hussein Obama.

Peter Luger Steakhouse (1887–) One of Brooklyn's most ancient and important institutions. The steak is mouthwatering, the bread basket is excellent, their German home fries are crunchy and delicious, but everything else kind of sucks . . . except the shrimp cocktail, which is decent but unremarkable. The waiters are generally gruff if not outright rude, the ambiance is stark, and the clientele skews heavily toward the white male patriarchy.

The Peter O'Toole Society takes its name from an informal association of people with double-penis names, such as Peter O'Toole, Jimmy Johnson, Woody Johnson . . . You get the picture: lots of Johnsons. We were in college and not terribly mature.

Reinsurance The reinsurance industry consists of insurance companies that insure other insurance companies. If you want to make lots of money and if the idea of living in Bermuda appeals to you, reinsurance is a field you may wish to pursue.

Trent Reznor (1965–) As a young man, I enjoyed his creepy-sexy, skin-crawling music videos and some of his angsty, light-industrial jams. He has since emerged as a bona fide scorer of films—some say his music saved the movie *The Social Network*.

Condoleezza Rice (1954–) A professor at Stanford University and gifted pianist, Condoleezza Rice was National Security Advisor under President George W. Bush at the time of the 9/11 attacks. She became Secretary of State in 2005, and it was later revealed that longtime boss of Libya, Muammar Gaddafi (who deserves his own Appendix entry but isn't getting one), had a huge crush on her.

Mitt Romney (1947–) A rich man who ran for president in 2012. Romney once transported Seamus, his family's (incontinent) Irish Setter, on a six-hundred-fifty-mile journey on top of his Chevy Caprice station wagon. Here's a fun Internet search: "Romney who let the dogs out."

Star and Buc Wild (Troi Torain: 1964–; Timothy Joseph: 1979–) Troi Torain aka Star founded the seminal magazine *Around the Way Connections*, served as a controversial and embattled hip-hop radio host, and authored *Objective Hate*. In 1995, he created an alter ego named Buc Wild to pen a monthly column in *The Source* back when the magazine was cool, sort of. Called "Reality Check," the column was the one voice of dissent in an otherwise ass-kissing morass of industry hype. The alter ego later came to life in the form of Star's younger half-brother, Timothy Joseph. Their subsequent media triumphs and misadventures are too numerous to mention here. I'm sure they're still hating away on the Internet somewhere . . .

Three Loco (2011–) A laugh-rap supergroup that consists of Dirt Nasty, Andy Milonakis, and Riff Raff.

Trading Places A 1983 movie starring Eddie Murphy, Dan Ackroyd, and Jamie Lee Curtis; directed by John Landis.

Alan Turing (1912–1954) This man's life and contribution to science defy the confines of this Appendix entry. Start by looking him up on Wikipedia, and go from there. Or see *The Imitation Game*.

John Varvatos (1955–) I don't know much about John Varvatos except he took over the old CBGB for his flagship store and also sells vintage stereo components there. Pretty cool, I guess. Evidently the man loves rock and roll. He also manages to sell worn-out-looking T-shirts for $228, so he must be a damn genius.

Pretty Hurts

Another one of her ambiguously set period pieces. Is it the '70s? The '80s? The '90s? (So glad we learned about anachronisms in English class! Comes in handy with Beyoncé videos.) Bey shows us the ugly side of beauty. Pains and pressures of being a woman in this superficial society. Backstage at the beauty contest, and it ain't pretty. Or if it is, it's a painful pretty. Waist cinching, booty spritzing, and teeth whitening. Alone at home wearing bunny ears and "gangsta" socks. Fat-shaming black albino choreographer. Wha? Beyoncé needs to slim down? I don't think so! Singing audition. White judges sitting in shadows. The beauty contest emcee is a very familiar-looking old white man in a tux jacket made of silver rubber.

Loneliness, despair, alienation.

Sisters throwing shade. Fights over hair dryers. Diet pills, bulimia, Botox, plastic surgery, spray tanning, damaged roots. Working out in clunky shoes on outdated home exercise equipment.

Thankfully a trophy-smashing fantasy sequence provides some release from this bleak view of the young and beautiful!

When the pageant is won by an emaciated freak whose face can only be described as otherworldly (and who appears to be the only contestant of color with lighter skin than Beyoncé?),

Bey's character appears relieved. Yes, I must remind myself this isn't Beyoncé in this video; she is portraying a character. Acting. Beyoncé is not Miss Third Ward; that's just the character she's playing.

Beauty shot of Bey with super short hair and makeup expertly applied to give the illusion of no makeup.

We finish with adorable (and seemingly authentic) video clip of Bey as a little girl accepting an award for "female pop vocalist," no doubt at a beauty pageant.

The Takeaway: it sucks to be beautiful.

Haunted

Okay it's getting creepy in here. Creepy TV monitors. Creepy 1950s domestic scenes with creepy Caucasian mannequin family. Ambiguous medical equipment. Grotesque opulence. A fire flashes alive in the fireplace and the video's title appears on the grainy screen of an ancient TV set: HAUNTED.

Oh, look! It's Beyoncé and her luggage in a cute little green convertible from some older, more glamorous era. She's driving along a winding coastal road to arrive at an opulent mansion. Uh-oh, I bet this is where all that creepy stuff is going on. No, wait, that's not her sexy black butler lighting her cigarette; he's a bellhop, and this is a hotel.

Bey takes one luscious drag and drops the cigarette to the marble floor, puts it out with the sole of her very expensive shoe, then makes her way up the winding stairs. With short platinum locks pasted to her head in dramatic waves like a rich white lesbian from the 1920s, she's got an elegant black pantsuit to match. Her complexion is a shade lighter than Madonna's. She makes her way through the hotel corridors, glancing into each room to glimpse surreal scenes that vary in degrees of creepiness. The first room offers a relatively innocent tableau of a young man wearing a letterman's jacket and a very large watch, getting his hair did by a sultry young woman, as Beyoncé's face looks on from the flatscreen TV behind them. She continues down the hallway and finally starts singing this creepy song. I mean, the Beyoncé on the TV screen sings. The 1920s lesbian Beyoncé walks silently through the halls.

More rooms, more weirdness, more creepy. Creepy white goth girl. Creepy white hairless cat in the clutches of a creepy old white goth lady. Creepy old white man with a face tattoo in a wheelchair. Shirtless tattooed young black men playing high-stakes poker and smoking cigars while a French maid serves them champagne.

This room not so creepy, kinda hot (except for the cigars). Weirdos wearing feathers and gas masks. Creepy white goth twins in matching striped jumpsuits and matching mismatched shoes. Glam strippers leaning against more monitors with Bey's singing face. Glam stripper straddling older businessman. Androgynous bubble bath. That creepy Caucasian mannequin family again. Sinewy black woman with short platinum hair, elaborate panties, and black stars over her nipples dancing with a big paintbrush and a bucket of black paint. Creepy black gangster dudes in white face.

When we get to the room with 1920s lesbian Bey on the bed and four pale white dancers with matching bobs and long-sleeve lingerie, slouching and crouching, spinning and grinding on the floor, I see we are finally getting to some choreography.

When I see that Bey has lost the pants from her pantsuit, and we begin cutting back to the other rooms to see all these creeps and assorted weirdos getting down and dirty with each other, I am reminded that Beyoncé isn't always suitable for children. (To be fair, this is one of six songs/videos on the album that is labeled "explicit".) Scenes ramp up to a freaky crescendo, TV screens are smashed, Beyoncé calmly exits, and the fire in the fireplace goes out.

The takeaway: White people are creepy; the whiter, the creepier. But black people can be creepy, too!

Drunk in Love (featuring Jay Z)

Honestly, when I saw the title of this song, I was imagining the word "Drunk" was being used as a metaphor for Love's intoxicating qualities. Boy, was I wrong. The song could have just as easily been called "Drunk and Horny." Okay, sometimes Beyoncé is *really* not suitable for young children. I'm not even comfortable with the message of this song being directed at *me*. Well, at least I'm old enough to know better. But I'm not so sure the same is true for all the other 17-year-olds out there.

I wish it were not the case, but I have a feeling that "Drunk in Love" is going to be one of the hits off this album. (Aren't her songs with Jay Z always hits?)

Here are my impressions. The ocean. Black-and-white beach scene. Bey meandering along the sand in sleepwear (or is it beachwear?), clutching one of her beauty trophies from the "Pretty Hurts" video. Dopey stares, improvised tai chi, and some sultry sand-grinding tell us she's in the mood for some inebriated boinking. She even slurs and stumbles over her lyrics—"swerving, surfing, swerfing"—she's really committing to this character!

Sparse arrangement. Strings and intermittent drums. The musical mood is airy, and this "drunken love" feels more detached and distant than intimate.

Uh-oh, here comes Jay Z rapping with a stagger in his swagger. Name checking his cognac (D'Ussé) and name-dropping his art collection (Warhol). It appears that even when drunk and alone on the beach with Beyoncé, this man has a difficult time ever making eye contact with his wife. Wait a second, what?! Was that an Ike Turner reference? Um, yep. "Eat the cake, Anna Mae!" refers to a scene from the movie *What's Love Got to Do with It?*, where Tina Turner's physically abusive husband forces her to eat a piece of cake in celebration of her solo success. I love you, Bey, but. This. Is. Not. Cool.

The takeaway: Bey can get every bit as freaky as Rhianna, and she's a blast to be with at the beach when she's drunk. Oh, and Jay Z is a very sensitive lover.

AFTERWORD

The glacial pace of publishing, even in this so-called Digital Age, is mind-boggling. We are writing this so-called "Afterword" at the last moment possible for it to appear in the hardcover first edition of *Little White Lies*—a book that revels in the immediacy of communicating through blogs, emails, texts, and tweets—more than four months before it will hit the shelves. The earliest you'll be reading it is February 2016, nearly two and a half years after we began the project. Blockbuster movies and their attending sequels have been conceived, written, produced, focus-grouped, and distributed to theaters in less time. Our first draft was due—er, we should say, submitted—on January 21, 2015: a full year before its release.

The constraints of our publishing schedule factored into our concerns about the timeliness of our book. We also considered this notion of timeliness in designing the arc of the plot. We wanted our book to be *timely*—that is, *of these times*. But we imagined that a book set in the "modern day" (an expression that feels outdated before, during, and after typing it) might feel outdated before it was even published, based solely on the protagonists' preferred social media platforms. Lacking Karl's supremely confident holiday-party prediction swagger, we couldn't be entirely sure if people would still be tweeting in February 2016.

So we decided to put a very specific time-stamp on our novel. This would allow us to reflect the times during which it was written, if not the times when it would be read. Our time-stamp decision also allowed us to incorporate "real-life" events into our fictional narrative. Through the course of writing the book—a collaborative process between the two of us and our editor Dan Ehrenhaft that involved a series of incremental deadlines (each one missed and extended at least once) and its own real-life cycle of texts, emails, and phone calls—we periodically tweaked the time line to adhere to school holidays, real world events, allusions to Shakespeare, and Beyoncé release dates. The time frame of the book loosely matches up with the time frame of its composition. The story begins one day before we signed our contracts, and ends in "Summer 2014"—just after Coretta has graduated from high school, and probably right around the time our manuscript was initially due.

Since then, however, we have witnessed (primarily through the lens of the Internet) a panoply of tragedies, outrages, head-scratchers, punch lines, absurdities—even the formation of a new political movement—that would have made perfect fodder for *Little White Lies*—both Coretta's fictional blog (and TV show, if it ever got off the ground!) as well as the real book you hold in your hands.

One of the biggest dilemmas we faced as we were completing the last chapters of the book was how, for example, to account for the tragedy in Ferguson, Missouri—wherein Michael Brown, an unarmed young black man, was shot and killed by Darren Wilson, a white police officer—and all the tumult that followed in its wake. Michael Brown was killed on August 9, 2014—months after our novel's action had ended, yet months before we completed our manuscript. How could we write a book addressing contemporary racial tensions and identity, we wondered, without acknowledging something we sensed at the time to be a potential catalyst for a shift in our nation's racial consciousness?

Many events since have begged the question, "What would Coretta have to say about this?"

What would she have to say about the Black Lives Matter movement? About the death of Freddie Gray and the ensuing protests in Baltimore? About Rachel Dolezal? About the massacre of nine black churchgoers in Charleston at the hands of a young white supremacist?

But this book, of course, was never intended to dwell in such unfathomable horror. At its heart, it is meant to be fun, humorous, provocative. On the other hand, comedy has its own dark side. In October 2014 (months after the final chapter of *Little White Lies* was closed, yet months before Karl's epilogue would be written), comedian Hannibal Buress called Bill Cosby a rapist during his stand-up act; the clip went viral; over the next several months more than 50 women came forward to accuse Cosby of drugging and raping them, with the alleged attacks dating back some 50 years; public support for Cosby steadily waned until July 2015, when a Philadelphia judge unsealed decade-old court transcripts in which Cosby admitted to having administered Quaaludes to young women as a means to take advantage of them sexually. Here was one of the most famous and successful black men in America—beloved for his comedy career and television masterpieces, revered and resented for his outspoken critiques of perceived failings within the black community—exposed as a hypocrite of the creepiest kind.

Coretta would no doubt have a lot to say about both Cosby and Buress, as would her parents. As would Karl.

They would have plenty to say, too, about the recent gravity-affirming freefall of Australian model-turned-rapper Iggy Azalea—after a series of her racist and homophobic tweets were dredged up from the not too distant past. On black twitter the *schadenfreude* was palpable.

And what about Terry Bollea aka Hulk Hogan, arguably the most famous professional wrestler of all time? As of late July 2015 he was entirely scrubbed from the official history of pro wrestling (have a look at the WWE web site and see if you can find him), after audio recordings surfaced where Bollea/Hogan privately declared, "I am a racist, to a point. F***ing n***ers."*

Way to go, Hulkster!

Inevitably there will be an untold number of *LWL*-worthy happenings, flare-ups, faux pas, showdowns, spectacles, controversies, and catastrophes over the days, months, years between now and the time you're reading these words—which, presumably, means you've read to The End. Well done.

We, the authors, have come to peace with the understanding that the fictional blog we created, written by a fictional character about real events, will not necessarily persevere beyond these pages. We can only hope that real-life people, young and old alike, will pick up where Coretta left off, and take to their own tumblrs, Facebook pages, YouTubes, Instagrams, or whatever the kids are using these days to communicate, to do what Coretta prescribed in her final words on television, and which Karl reiterated at the end of his epilogue: seek and empower truth and justice; recognize and oppose injustice and deception.

Thank you for reading.

—Brianna Baker and F. Bowman Hastie III

---

* Whereas our protagonists would likely eschew the use of asterisks to bowdlerize such words, Karl and Coretta lacked our good fortune of having a professional editor.

ACKNOWLEDGMENTS

The authors would like to thank: Dan, Bronwen, Rachel, Meredith, and the entire Soho Teen team; Kaya and Amaechi; Dave; each other; and you the reader.

Thanks also to Rita Williams-Garcia and Michael Render aka Killer Mike, and Dorian Warren for their early support.

Brianna Baker would like thank: Dad, Lauren, Evan, Alek, Kelly, Nic, Jmiah, Walt, Jean, Blair, Punam, Gladyse, Steven, Joan, my manager Brian Stern at AGI Entertainment Media and Management, and Kristyn Keene at ICM.

F. Bowman Hastie III would like to thank: Mom, Dad, Matt, Amelie, John, Katie & Georgia, Tillie & Doc, Jay, Gordon, Shaina, Sasha, Stephen, Ricardo, AK & Family, smarcus, Darien, Fred, Kristen, Tyler, Chris & Anne, Sean, Dirk, Andy & Jack, Diane, Pollack, Jaishri, Reema, Courtney & Martin, Mira, Ramsey & Eric, Knuckles, and my agent Don Fehr at Trident Media Group. Special gratitude goes to IBC, Willard Moan, low-fi, Whizzy, Dreamkillers, Bottom Feeders, Nappy G, The 9-Inch Whales, Dred Scott Trio, T-n-T, Zelly Rock, Run-DMC, LL Cool J, The Beastie Boys, N.W.A., Public Enemy, Too $hort, The Jungle Brothers, Schoolly D, Eric B. & Rakim, Geto Boys, Kool G Rap, Big Daddy Kane,

Slick Rick, BDP, De La Soul, EPMD, A Tribe Called Quest, Brand Nubian, X Clan, Sir Fresh & DJ Critical, M.C. Nikke and DJ Rap N Scratch, Audio Two, MC Lyte, Positive K, Redman, Snoop Doggy Dogg, Kill Dog E, Domino, Nas, Outkast, Cypress Hill, Wu-Tang, Killah Priest, Biggie, Lil' Kim, The Click, DMX, Del, Kool Keith, The Pharcyde, Freestyle Fellowship, Organized Konfusion, Smoothe Da Hustler and Trigga tha Gambler, Eminem, Missy Elliot, Blackalicious, Jay-Z, Kanye, Lil Wayne, Nicki Minaj, Drake, Three Loco, Kendrick Lamar, Lil Dicky, Run The Jewels, Mr. Magic & Marley Marl, DJ Chuck Chillout, Kool DJ Red Alert, Teddy Tedd & Special K (Audio 2), DNA & Hank Love, Stretch & Bobbito.